TIDAL WATERS

First published by Charco Press 2024
Charco Press Ltd., Office 59, 44-46 Morningside Road, Edinburgh
EH10 4BF

Copyright © Velia Vidal, 2020
First published in Spanish as *Aguas de estuario* (Bogotá: Laguna)
English translation copyright © Annie McDermott, 2024

The rights of Velia Vidal to be identified as the author of this work and of Annie McDermott
to be identified as the translator of this work have been asserted by them in accordance with
the Copyright, Designs and Patents Act 1988.

Work published with support from the Reading Colombia Translation Support Programme /
Obra editada con apoyo del programa Reading Colombia, cofinanciación a la traducción

A CIP catalogue record for this book is available
from the British Library.

ISBN: 9781913867768
e-book: 9781913867775

www.charcopress.com

Edited by Fionn Petch
Cover designed by Pablo Font
Typeset by Laura Jones-Rivera
Proofread by Fiona Mackintosh

Velia Vidal

TIDAL WATERS

Translated by
Annie McDermott

CHARCO PRESS

FOREWORD

by
Djamila Ribeiro

The first time I met Velia Vidal was at the Hay Festival in Cartagena de Indias, in January 2022. She had just become the first Afro-Colombian woman writer to receive a grant from the Colombian Ministry of Culture for the publication of her book Aguas de estuario, the fundamental work of literature that occupies the following pages. It was also in 2022 that Velia Vidal was selected by the BBC as one of the world's most influential and inspiring women. We were together in that walled city, as beautiful as it is shot through with inequalities of race, class, and gender, and there I felt for the first time the warmth of her writing and the wisdom of her words spoken in favour of the democratization of reading and the improvement in the quality of life of the Afro-Colombian community.

Before presenting the author's work, I think it is worthwhile reflecting on what Lélia González has called 'Amefrican' identity. It is necessary to find a political publishing project that focuses on disseminating great literature written by black women from South America. As a Brazilian, I know that my country has to emerge from its condition as a linguistic island in the continent and look around it, and not only to the north. With this movement, we will see South American blackness beating strong-ly through literary initiatives that are fundamental to understanding our own identity, which united us when our ancestors were kidnapped and brought to this continent by force. It united us again when we lived, over the past century and up to the present day, under the false idea of racial democracy, an illusion that claims the situation of the black population in South America is one big party, without apartheids.

Why did we begin by bringing and her Aguas de Estuario to Brazil? For us women at the Sello Sueli Carneiro and the Colección Femenismos Plurales, coordinated by myself and published by the brave Jandaíra house, Velia Vidal's work has been profoundly inspiring. To date, our initiative has published over twenty books, with over a dozen of black Brazilian woman authors, and hundreds of thousands of books sold. On this journey which begins in the coming pages, we will swap ideas with the project dreamt up by Velia, which independently pursues her dream of democratizing books, writing and reading for Afro-Latin Americans.

Together with the author we will explore Chocó, a department in Colombia's north-west with coasts on both the Pacific and the Caribbean, and where the great majority of people are black. The proud people of Chocó have shaped Afro-Colombian culture over many years. The capital is Quibdó, from where Vidal writes most of the letters that make up this novel, while others introduce us to her birthplace, Bahía Solano, and take us on a tour of a part of Colombia that needs to be much better known to everyone.

Through this book we will discover Velia's dreams, her sources of inspiration, and her determination to make a success of her brave Motete initiative, which carries out work that is recognised in the community and internationally as transformative, based on the democratisation of reading, literacy and the organisation of literary fairs to promote black literature, among many other projects.

Velia Vidal's debut in Brazil was a highlight in the association between Editora Jandaíra and Feminismos Plurais and opened a bridge between the diasporas in Brazil and Colombia, an exchange that is providing readers with great opportunities for intellectual enrichment.

It is great news that Velia Vidal is now able to bring Tidal Waters to English-speaking readers thanks to Charco Press. This is a real chance for the specific characteristics of Afro-Colombian identities in particular, and Afro-Latin American in general, for our Amefrican identity, to become better known and understood in other latitudes.

Happy reading!

Djamila Ribeiro
São Paulo
20th May 2023.

To my recipient,
simply for being there

Medellín, 25 May 2015

You know me, I'm just like the Pacific. I can be calm one minute and then suddenly break into great powerful waves, which crash down and end up changing the landscape. The things that happen to people, the cycles of the moon, or simply life itself, have led me to a decision that many people find strange, though to us it seems almost obvious. And I want to tell you about it in advance.

As of the first week of July, my husband, my cats and I will no longer live in Medellín. We'll be residents of Bahía Solano. We're going to live the dream at the same time as building it.

I'd like to tell you all this in person, to see your face as I speak, and for you to see mine. I so enjoy writing to you, but looking at you as I speak is like reading you twice over.

I'll tell you a bit more:

We decided a couple of years ago that we were going to go back. And last year we made a five-year plan, which we went on fine-tuning. My work in Medellín was going well, and we decided my husband would also look for a job, while he carried on selling the fish we brought to the city from Bahía Solano.

Well, my husband didn't find a job and I started to get bored of mine. Then Juana's mother was diagnosed with late-stage cancer and Luis Miguel had that heart attack, and I took it all very seriously and said: I can't be anywhere I'm bored; we need to do things every day if we want to be happy and at peace when it's our time to go, whatever it is that brings us peace. So I decided to quit. And what followed was a search for something that made me happier, or that brought me peace, because over time I've discovered that's what happiness is: feeling at peace and free of unfinished business, including deferred dreams.

On top of all this, as you well know, there's my endocrinologist's insistence that I cut down on stress, to see if that helps with my Graves' disease. My husband pointed out that we didn't need to wait five years to leave; we could put everything together as we were living it. And the basics would have to be sorted out either there or here. The advantage would be that there, we'd have the sea to soothe us whenever things got tricky. We set about doing the sums, considering our responsibilities, and everything started to flow. That seemed like a good sign, so we decided to leave.

We have enough money to get by for a couple of months, and now we're weighing up different business ideas, ready to invest and get to work.

Essentially, the dream has always involved this:

Living simply, being near the sea, being near my grandmother again (this one's mine, but my husband supports it because he knows how much it means to me), building a sustainable house, continuing to strengthen this family of ours, having time to read and write, serving our neighbours (there are many ways of serving), having a steady income that means we can afford this life and all it involves (such as travelling whenever necessary).

Now you can make your own mind up about the reasons for this change; if it's about aspiration, or desire.

I'd like us to have a coffee together before I go. To do our thing of meeting up and reading, and so I can give you a hug; after all, it's not every day that a person moves cities, especially after fifteen years in the same place.

Kisses,
    Vel

H_{ey,}

I realise it's months since I last wrote to you. Maybe that brief phone conversation in September was enough, the day I told you I was in hospital with a bacterial infection I picked up in Litoral de San Juan. You were so quick to call that I wasn't sure if you'd read my message properly. I think later I messaged to say I'd been discharged and was leaving town again, after eleven days in hospital. A twenty-four-hour visit to see my husband became a stay full of antibiotics, because my twenty years living outside Chocó have made me weak.

So far here, as well as the bacterial infection that sent me to hospital, I've had chikungunya disease, a fungal infection, and patches of melasma on my face. As if I didn't have enough with my Graves' disease and the fatigue, breathlessness and racing heart it sometimes causes.

Speaking of which, I should tell you that in response to the test results I emailed to Olga, my endocrinologist, last month from Medellín, she said: 'Please don't ever go back there – stay in Chocó.'

I was in Pizarro last week – you can see in the photos. It's right where the Baudó river meets the Pacific, and it's where I ended my three months of adventures through Chocó. Getting there isn't easy: two hours by car from Quibdó to Istmina, then nearly three hours on a terrible road from Istmina to Puerto Meluk, and another two and a half along the Baudó by boat. I travelled around some of Upper San Juan, and Middle and Lower Baudó. A part of Chocó I'd never been to before. It was fascinating to recognise new landscapes in this place that's so deeply mine, but which so much remains for me to explore. The waters of the Baudó river, which I found so enigmatic; the vast Pizarro mangroves. And the lonely villages emptied out by pressure from armed groups.

It was painful as well. I came across a case of mismanagement involving children's food. I had to be at my most level-headed, confront the situation and start putting it right. I'm only now experiencing the ugly, difficult side of overseeing the School Food Programme. I have a lot to learn. Luckily I was near the sea, and could feel its strength. And luckily in that same place I met extraordinary, honest, determined people.

I haven't really explained how I ended up doing this work, but I don't want to go into all that now.

Kisses,
    Velia

Bahía Solano, 31 October 2015

My work overseeing the food programme took me to Juradó. I got back yesterday; I'm now in Bahía Solano. In Juradó I met Simón and Jodier.

Simón paints half his face red because his mum taught him he could trick the devil that way and then the devil wouldn't be able to scare him. When he grows up, Simón, who's nine, wants to be a soldier. Simón likes jagua – indigenous body paint – but Jodier doesn't. Jodier is eight and when he grows up he wants to be happy. Jodier and Simón are cousins. They live in Buenavista, an indigenous community on the banks of the Jampabadó river, very near the border with Panama.

Jodier and Simón gave me the wooden batea for gold-panning, a gift from the whole community. A batea that was made by an old man, and for many years was used to mix fermented corn to make chicha. My batea travelled back with me to the municipal capital of Juradó, and then for over two hours by boat to Bahía Solano, and soon it will find a space in my house. A house that hasn't been built yet, but where spaces for stories are guaranteed.

Talking to Simón about jagua made me think about my own demons, and I wonder about yours as well, because we all have our demons. Simón uses jagua; how do we scare our demons away? How do you scare yours?

Quibdó, 12 February 2016

There's something I call *absence of sea*. It's a particular sensation, a series of singular emotions that take hold when it's a long time since I last saw the sea. It's a kind of yearning, and so physical – I notice it on my skin – that you could say it's like getting the shivers. It makes me feel almost homesick, and on the verge of sadness, even if it's a happy time. Then my every pore starts crying out, and I know for sure that what I'm missing is the sea. Gazing at each other, touching each other: me and the sea. So whenever I have that sensation I need to hurry to the nearest place where we can be reunited at last. Absence of sea has made me travel to Capurganá, to Necoclí and, of course, to Bahía Solano on several occasions.

I haven't written to you for a long time. I'm not quite sure why not, but I'm here now because I'm beginning to feel something similar to absence of sea. In this case it's a kind of absence of you. I'll try to bring you up to speed with what's been going on.

While I was in Juradó, I decided to come and live in Quibdó. Five days after that last letter I wrote you, I sorted out the few things I had in Bahía and travelled to Quibdó. I rented a flat in the centre, and my husband finally sent over all the stuff from Medellín.

I'd already brought my cats, and now it's the three of us, Mandarina, Sasha and me, in this sweltering city on the banks of the Atrato. I hadn't planned to come back here. I don't have the best memories of it from my childhood, but a lot of things have changed since then, not in Quibdó but in me, so that now I see it differently.

As of four days ago I'm the new head of communications at the Chocó Chamber of Commerce. It sounds as if I've thrown out my shorts and flip-flops and shut myself up in an office, but that's not how it is. This is a great opportunity that makes the dream house by the sea feel much closer, and in the meantime lets me serve the land I come from.

Tomorrow I start a diploma in reading promotion, and with it my project, Motete. We've chosen three areas of Quibdó where I'll start running the workshops.

Life is still coloured green and blue. I haven't seen the sea since December, partly because we're going to Brazil in August, for the Olympics, which we've dreamt of doing for years, so we're budgeting for that. We have tickets now, and accommodation. We're doing well. So I've put off a couple of encounters with the sea here, in order to meet it in August in Rio de Janeiro.

Microbusinesses Colombia got in touch to ask me to help with some comms. On Monday, someone will visit from Medellín, the person I'm usually in touch with. I'll let you know how it goes. I enjoy it a lot.

Hugs,
    Vel

Quibdó, 13 April 2016

I would have liked to talk to you yesterday. I needed a broader perspective and the voice of someone wiser than me – and you're comfortably into that category. There was a choice I had to make: carry on offering communications services (separately to my work in the Chamber) as a way of funding reading promotion, or focus on reading promotion and work out a way for it to fund itself?

The communications seed is growing very quickly. It's something people need in the region and I have the tools to provide a good service. Still, it's beginning to take time away from my new love – Motete, that is, and reading promotion, which has become an obsession.

I spoke to Juangui, I listened to myself and I listened to him, and his words helped me remember what happens when I take on too many things that distance me from what I came here for, namely the chance to devote myself to what I love the most, to the things that fill my soul. You also know what happens to me, you know I get sick, and depressed, that I get into a state and before I know it I'm not even strong enough to get out of bed.

These have been months without many dualities. So this one is welcome. Love wins in the end, as it always must. I won't give in to the temptation to be a great comms specialist or start the comms company that Chocó needs. I'll keep working at being Seño Velia, who reads stories and who people look at (most people here don't see you, they look at you. They say, for example: I looked at you yesterday when you were at the market) in the neighbourhood with her motete full of books, because she's convinced that's how we can turn all this around.

I'm sending you love and I'd love to see you. I hope the day comes soon; for a long time now I've been nurturing the idea of seeing you in person. The last time I wrote, you said we should meet up when I was next in Medellín, but I haven't been back. I haven't needed to. My life is here now, and although my husband isn't yet living with me full-time, he tries to come fairly often. That means going to Medellín is no longer such a priority, but I'd definitely like to go, to see you, to see Juana, Liliana, Luis Miguel, Juangui, so many friends I haven't seen for ages. I suppose this is what big life changes are like.

Hugs,
     Vel

Quibdó, 6 June 2016

Last week was the second teachers' club session at the Bank of the Republic. Since the bank has a limited budget, they suggested I do just one hour a week, but I, excited to have nine or ten teachers interested, give them two hours anyway. Let the bank pay what it can.

Our club includes two strands of work: training as readers and training as reading promoters. It turns out the teachers aren't readers; you wouldn't believe how low their level is. So it was a real cause for celebration when we managed to read three stories in our session.

We did an exercise involving reading aloud and I taught them a bit about voice control, based on my experience giving presentations. It's never been so satisfying to use that knowledge and experience. I feel very happy.

Tomorrow I have an appointment with the headteacher of my old school. They have a newly refurbished library there, which is also a bit underused. I want it to be the setting for the crónica-reading club (for teenagers) and the children's club. If they say yes, I'll begin at least one of the two this coming week.

For teacher training week, someone suggested I give a talk about the importance of reading to the teachers from a school on the banks of the Quito river, in the settlement of San Isidro. I hope I can do it – I think it would be great.

And so this story is coming together. This basket, this Motete, is filling up. The slogan for my project is 'Contenidos que tejen' – contents that weave – and every day I like it more. Every day I realise that these contents are weaving fulfilment and happiness within me. Do you know what a motete is yet? I think I sent you a photo. It's basically a basket used by indigenous people for carrying food, with a strap that goes over the head. 'Motete' is what we call those baskets on the North Pacific coast (Bahía Solano, Juradó, Nuquí) and in Panama. The thing is, motetes have always been used to carry food for the body: plantains, bushmeat, fish. Our idea is to fill them with food for the soul: art, culture, books. And just as motetes are woven by hand, I thought these new contents would also form a fabric: the fabric of society, of community, the fabric of souls.

At some point – sooner than you think – I'll need you, so we can keep on weaving a big motete and keep on filling it up.

I haven't seen the sea since December and I miss it, of course. This is a long, sustained absence of sea, but also one that I've chosen. I'm feeling it deeply. However, I'm surer by the day that the sea is inside me; it's part of what moves me to do this work.

It's been raining a lot. The downpours are so particular to this jungle, and so heavy, that sometimes I find them impossible to describe. I believe in the power of this rain and these seas.

Soon it'll be a year since I arrived here. And soon we'll see each other again; I'm finally travelling to your city and we'll be able to have breakfast together. It's so beautiful to describe days without any boredom.

Those that have gone by and those yet to come.

Lots of love,
    Seño Velia

What are you trying to do? Take up what little space in my heart wasn't already yours?

Well, you've succeeded. You've filled my whole heart, you've won it all, by going out of your way to help us take Dayana to Medellín for her birthday. I've learned here that a lot of things that many people find quite ordinary, for others are a great gift. Ana wanted her daughter to take a plane for the first time, to see a city with her own eyes. You and various other friends made it possible.

The gift might seem to have been for other people, but deep down it was a great gift to me. Knowing I can count on you, knowing I can count on so many friends who have put themselves, their families and their resources at my disposal to help make this dream come true.

Did you know you're all telling me you love me very much?

A sea of thanks.

Kisses and hugs,
    Vel

Quibdó, 23 June 2016

Travelling along a stretch of the Quito river one day with forty teachers and forty-five books, meeting three women a couple of days later to discuss reading promotion in Chocó, then getting a phone call from a mother to check that the women's and children's clubs start on Saturday. This is how I'm reading another Chocó, discovering another story. I'm rereading Velia and discovering personality traits that feel new.

Characters appear who really are writing a new story between the water and the jungle. The idea of development is dealt with in a paragraph that seems almost incidental, and the characters who take centre stage in most things we read aren't even mentioned in these new texts.

Some months ago I was saying with total certainty that Chocó is where I belong in the world, the place I need to be, my base, from which I can go anywhere and still always return, and where I feel complete even though it lacks so many things, and I wasn't wrong. Now I know, too, that being Seño Velia is my mission on this earth; it's like it's what I was born to do.

I don't know if I mentioned this specifically, perhaps not in a letter, though maybe when we met up before I left to come and live here for good, but part of what pushed me to make this radical life change was the need to feel that my existence had meaning, that I was spending each day doing something I cared about and could feel proud of at the end of my life. And that's just what I've found in being Seño Velia, the woman who has meetings with people about books, who tries to motivate children to love reading and books as much as she does, and who supports the teachers.

I spent almost all of Sunday with my dad. We cooked together, talked, watched the rain, drank coffee. This is the place in the universe where everything I love can come together on a single page, everything that fills my soul, everything that makes me happy – which is also, as you know, everything that brings me calm.

In forty days I'm going to have breakfast with you and in forty-one I'm going to visit a different country for the first time, where I'll find another sea, and sports, and new children's books with African-heritage characters. Half an hour from here, all I could ever need.

Have a nice day.

Kisses,
Vel

P.S. Writing to you means telling myself the story of my life in a different tone. I find it soothing as well. It's a way of taking a step back and seeing what I am and what I do from a distance, which shows how insignificant some of the things are that overwhelm me in everyday life. When you say that what I write to you brightens your days, you brighten mine in return. Writing, then, becomes like a circle of joy between us.

Quibdó, 4 July 2016

I don't know if you remember exactly when we met. I think it was the day I went to your office with Luis Miguel. We were going to ask for your support with an event. I was really nervous because I was new and learning the ropes – Miguel wanted to show me how the process of getting culture funding worked. You seemed like a friendly, approachable guy, which of course you are. You gave me your card and said I could email you to make arrangements. There was no way of knowing that that business meeting would turn into a friendship.

I'm not sure, but I think when the support eventually materialised, you no longer worked for that company. But by then this friendship of ours had already begun. Still in the early stages; we wouldn't have called it a friendship.

There have been some moments of proximity, and others – the majority – of distance. A constant connection that's difficult to name, but it's a difficulty I'm not interested in overcoming. I don't think everything needs to have an accepted, validated name. This is a connection I feel and it moves me to seek you out, to write to you, to remember you. I only need to feel it to know it's there.

July 3rd marked 366 days since I came here from Medellín. It's 366 because this is a leap year. A year of being far away. And I want to tell you, my dear friend, that you've never felt so close by.

This year I've travelled a lot, over rivers and seas, down unpaved roads, through the middle of the jungle, with rain overhead or scorching sun. I've followed this path and found what so far I think is my purpose in life. I've run a marathon through my emotions, and my ways of dealing with them. And this whole year I've felt you with me, very close.

I think you know better than most the details of what I've found on these journeys. I've been able to share with you the things I've seen, and what's more, you've been complicit in my adventures.

As well as dedicating this year to everything I've learned and to the people who have become part of my life, I dedicate it to you. To your constant companionship, to the replies I know will come, and which encourage me so much. To the perfectly ordered words filled with our love for each other.

Perhaps it sounds bold to talk about love like that, but you see, I've stopped being afraid of taking risks that only ever translate into happiness.

This place, intangible and yet so real, is like a harbour for my words. As you know, I live on a sea, and I've got into the habit of coming back here to rest and set down a little of my soul. You have become one of my ports.

I want to keep coming back here, where my only investment is time, and receive in return some big smiles I can savour again and again, simply by rereading. I also receive the wonderful prospect of seeing you in person, and refilling these words with your face and your voice – in other words, with you.

Kisses,
    Veliamar

Medellín, 1 August 2016

I've been reflecting on what you said yesterday at breakfast and I think it's true. It makes no sense to be embarrassed about sharing my writing with you, since by now you're so good at reading what I'm really saying between the lines.

I think I'm afraid: afraid to let the characters I've created in those stories belong to anyone other than me. Even though they were born to belong to children. I'm a bit nervous about what might happen if these characters are illustrated, interpreted by the hand of an artist, and become characters in a book that many people can touch. But I suppose that's an important part of writing.

I so enjoyed filling up on your voice.

Laughing together, feeling that you were uncovering my true story amid the flurry of words, discussing our bracelets and where each one came from, hearing about you. Looking at one another. That's what happiness is.

Lots of love.

Quibdó, 30 August 2016

When I was in Rio de Janeiro, a person I barely know shared a call for applications with me on Twitter. Something made me apply. And yesterday I found out that I'm one of the twenty-four people who will take the Pacific Diploma in Creative Writing, with all expenses paid. So I'll spend a week in Tumaco, then next month a week in a city in Cauca, then in Valle and finally in Chocó, working with two authors to write texts based on this jungle, these two seas and this Pacific perspective which, I'm sure, involves big brown eyes.

There were various selection criteria, and I had to send an example of my previous writing which showed literary quality and a link with the Pacific as the territory we inhabit. So I sent the story about Marinela and her curly hair moving in time with the breeze, which I shared with you a while ago, and back came this opportunity. Ninety-four people applied. It's a real privilege.

I don't know if it's going to make me a great writer. I know I'll have the pleasure of becoming more involved in the Pacific, and that I'll be pushed to leap, with my writing in my arms, into a vast sea of advice, criticism, exposure. I'll be able to grow. And what's more, as a result of the process, something I write will be published. Can you believe it? A chapbook will reach you and in it will be a text written by me.

It's scary. I'm sometimes surprised by how quickly dreams come true.

I have a lot of things to decide and sort out. I still don't even know if the Chamber will let me take the time off. But I've decided I'm going to do it all the same. And in the meantime I'll focus on more important decisions, such as whether to write as Velia Vidal Romero or as Veliamar. Amar and mar, love and the sea. Which name do you prefer?

Kisses,
    Vel

Dear friend,

I've been especially keen to write to you since last week, but the moment never arrived. Maybe my keenness has to do with my decision to add a bit more weight to this space than it's taken so far. I suppose I'm like Anansi, the spider, who once he's spun his web decides to put it to the test, and since he's a spider who tells stories, the only way of testing what he's spun is with other, heavier stories. Well, I'll risk testing this web we've been spinning out of words for a very long time now.

As so often, there's no good explanation for this, but if I wanted to find a reason why I'm bringing what I'm now bringing into this space, and adding the weight of new, personal things, I'd say it's because it feels like a safe harbour.

Testing the web might break it, but it might also make it stronger. We'll see, my dear friend. For now, here goes:

If I wanted to describe this trip in a single word, I'd say 'nakedness'. More than anything, the Pacific Diploma in Creative Writing has abruptly exposed my timid intention of becoming a writer. I had to strip naked and tell myself my truths about embarking on such a journey, and in this first session, as usual when a person undresses for the first time, I felt awkward, judged, even though there was no judgement from the others. I felt as if my ability to seriously confront the work of writing and even the act of reading was being questioned. But in the end, I fell in love with that awkwardness. I discovered that it's a good starting point, or, even if I find that it never goes away, that it's a good place for stretching your mind, emotions and literary devices to the fullest, until you can say what you want your words to say, as tunefully as a well-played marimba.

In Tumaco I revealed my body. Who would have thought that so many miles south would be the setting for a meeting with a lover? Strange, magical things often happen to me, and it seems this is no exception.

I first met this lover some years ago, and since then, counting the night in Tumaco, we've only slept together three times. Persisting in the idea that we've been lovers is more down to us intending to love each other whenever we get the chance, and always wanting each other, and understanding that our connection isn't only intellectual or based on shared interests but instead exists in the body. Unluckily, or perhaps luckily, our moments together have been few and far between, and to my surprise, the surprise of my lover and thanks to life's twists and turns, each encounter has had a different setting, a long way away from the last one.

For a while now I've felt our story was nearing its end: although we had a brief opportunity several months ago, I wouldn't even kiss him – this is how people are with lovers sometimes. So I didn't know why in Tumaco I felt so sure that I wanted to. My husband asked the same thing: why did I want to in Tumaco, when I hadn't taken any opportunities before that? Why had I said I didn't want to sleep with him again and then ended up deciding to do it?

You're probably wondering why my husband knows about all this, so I'll quickly try to explain. We're not exactly an open couple; we're a strange invention that's very particular to us, in which these kinds of things happen. I'd say this invention is the result of many conversations, misunderstandings and infidelities that we've been able to address and which have made us accept how implausible it is to love just one person for all eternity. We decided to stay together on the basis that it's possible to build a life together while also admitting that sometimes other people appear who we want to have sex with, and that there's no reason for that to disrupt our shared life. We've also agreed to discuss the things that happen to us. The way we see it, much of what feeds these extramarital affairs is the mystery. Keeping them secret makes them seem more dramatic and momentous, when really they're nothing but human stories, experiences that everyone has.

Going back to what happened in Tumaco, I think what decided me was the curious coincidence of it all, and wanting to accept the cards life had played me. I'd had no idea I'd receive a grant to attend a course in the Pacific, beginning in Tumaco; and I'd had no idea my old lover would be in that beautiful port town on the southern border on the same days as me, or that our schedules would allow this encounter to take place. It's not often life makes such a curious move, and who was I to turn down the invitation?

I discovered, however, that life had plenty more in store for me than that. My lover came to my room sooner than I expected. I was already naked, but because I was about to shower; he knocked on the door and I went to answer, covering myself slightly in case there was anyone else in the corridor. I made it into the shower, and then dried myself and pressed my body to his, which was already naked in bed. With its language of wetness, my woman's body told me how easy it would be and then I gave myself over to the sensations produced by his skin, skin whose marks spoke of the years of life that stand between us. All the while I was asking myself – and I even asked him – how it could be that despite so much time and so much distance there still remained so much desire. I also thought about the absurdity of this commitment-free bond, of this desire in the midst of so much absence and how little it generally crosses my mind.

Next came the caresses, the odd unusual position, the orgasms – one each, in the interests of accuracy – and then, just like that, it was over. We chatted a bit, about Tumaco, about the curious hand life had dealt us. Then, when my eyes were beginning to close, he decided we'd end the night apart, gave me a couple of kisses on the lips to which I couldn't respond, perhaps from tiredness, or perhaps because I knew it was the end.

What began on my phone out of the blue has ended the same way. So far there's been no 'Good journey home!', no 'Did you get back okay?', not even a tentative message to say 'Hi'. His name shows up on the list of active users on Facebook chat, but my fingers, which move like butterflies when they feel like writing, want only to be still.

Back home, all I could say to my husband was: 'I won't tell you I didn't enjoy it, but it wasn't all that. I think it was the end of the story.'

'And how do you feel about that?' he asked.

'Completely fine. I think it was time. These years have been enough, even if we only slept together three times. Nothing lasts forever. Or maybe it's time for a new lover to take his place.'

In Tumaco I decided to lay myself bare, here, with you. I had an urge to write about this way of seeing the world, of feeling with my body, of being with other men without ever leaving the comfortable, pleasant space of my marriage. Perhaps, as I peel back the layers in these letters, I will also uncover what's at the heart of all this, and find one more pleasure in this beautiful freedom. As I've said before, this feels like a safe harbour, where I can leave these things for the sole purpose of leaving them. I know it also means revealing myself to you, which is a risk – but, needless to say, one I've already decided to take.

Hugs,
Vel

Quibdó, 20 October 2016

Dear friend,

I have lots of things to tell you. For example, I decided to quit my job. I promise to write soon about Motete and all those practical life decisions. But the thing is, I can't resist the stories that feel more like poetry. I'd rather give you the verse than the prose of this life, which after all, in verse or prose, is so full of excitement.

As I said, I wrote you a letter in Guapi and read it out in public. I did it for the challenge of letting go of what I write, of understanding that writing belongs to other people and isn't some kind of precious treasure. It's one of the tasks of the Pacific Diploma.

Of course, my letters to you aren't meant to be published, but two important things came together: one is that if I'm told, 'Write a letter', my first thought is of you; and the other is that it was a real leap of faith to share something in public that contains my soul. It was a chance to confront my fear of laying myself bare through my writing. I confess my cheeks were burning and my tongue felt heavy as I read, but at the same time it was like being here, in this place that fills me with joy and peace, and then it was really special. A very important step in becoming a writer.

Thank you for being there, even without knowing it.

Our letter only covers the first two days of the trip. It doesn't mention, for example, that I went to Gorgona, saw whales again and it was like the first time: I heard their song as I was snorkelling and admiring the fish in the coral reef. It's deeply painful to see the ruins of the prison on the island, but life-affirming the way it's all being swallowed by nature.

I ended the week in hospital, with what seemed to be food poisoning. The sanitary conditions aren't good and by the looks of it I still have a city-dweller's stomach.

My soul was full on my return. Brimming with new places and faces, brimming with things I'd learned, with landscapes, with the Pacific. Here's the letter:

Dear friend,

As you know, I'm in Guapi. The photos I send from my phone usually tell you the news before my letters do. As you rightly said in response to the photos I sent, Guapi is beautiful; you'll have guessed that I feel at home here as well, because of the sea, the jungle, the seafood, the water, the other black people. I'm very surprised by how many things such distant places can have in common. But after all, that must be why I'm so happy here: I'm finding so much of my Chocó, so much of my place in the world, so much of myself.

Discovering this side of the Pacific also means venturing behind various stories, and finding words I can use to talk about it. In a way, it's the struggle to say what seems unsayable.

If I had to choose a word to describe what I've experienced in Guapi over the past two days, it would definitely be 'resistance'. It's easy to think this relates to it being a black community; resistance seems to be the territory of women, gay people and black people. But here I've experienced it differently.

The Guapi river is big. It reminded me of the San Juan, especially where it passes through Docordó – that is, when it's flowing down one of its arms into the Pacific. At that point, the river flows backwards. The powerful Pacific tides force it to do something that rivers aren't supposed to do, and the water flowing downhill seems to go back on itself. But the river refuses to stop being a river: it keeps its shape, its colour, and yet it flows the other way, though not without a fight. At times, this resistance seems to leave it in a kind of suspense. I think it's when the tide stops rising and begins to fall; you might find that it's not stillness but resistance.

The Pacific tries to penetrate these rivers with its saltwater, and they resist that too. The Guapi river has a slight taste of the sea, but it also tastes of the Guapi river.

Yesterday, after we'd arrived and spent some time enjoying the river scenery, we spoke with three representatives from a corporation called Chiyangua. For twenty-two years they've been working with the communities in Guapi, particularly the women; among many other things, they found in the women's wooden planters a kind of resistance, and have brought back the practice of growing medicinal, aromatic and culinary herbs like sawtooth coriander or pennyroyal, which had previously been lost. They have recovered forgotten traditional recipes. They fight to keep what they are and what they know from disappearing; they fight against losing their scents and flavours, and with them their way of life.

After a seafood lunch – no need to tell you how much I enjoyed that – we went to visit a community in the south called Chico Pérez. You have to cross a canal that was built through the mangroves as a quicker route to the inlet, then you reach the bay, and although you don't quite come face-to-face with the sea, you do join up with its waters.

Chico Pérez is called that because the surname of its founder was Anchico. The Anchicos are dead now, or many of them have left. Very few fishermen still live here, but the town is resisting the loss of its fishing tradition. Boats from Ecuador no longer come for the piangua oysters, but you still see the oysters stored beneath the houses on stilts in the mangrove swamp, to keep them alive until there are enough to sell to a middle-man who takes them to Ecuador.

The cold room is no longer in use, and mining activity means there are fewer and fewer shellfish, and therefore fewer young people who want to be fishermen. But in the mornings the catch of gualajos and corvinas comes in and is shared among the forty-five families in the community, and before midday the scent of langoustines in coconut sauce reminds you that the flavours of the seafood on Colombia's South Pacific coast are here to stay.

In the afternoon, one or other of the neighbours spends hours repairing the fishing nets that have been broken by the engines. Stitch by stitch, they resist hanging these nets up for good; they know the sea can still make fishermen of them.

Near the dock, on a little island in the mangroves, a FARC flag flutters in the breeze. They still have a presence here, a presence that holds out in Chico Pérez, in Guapi, even if the rest of the country thinks we've almost got rid of them. All you can see is the flag. We didn't see anyone carrying a gun, but that flag says it all. It's enough of a symbol to tell us they're here, and that just like the flag which no one dares to take down, and which ripples in time with the Pacific breeze, they're not going anywhere.

My dear friend, neither the Pacific tide nor the currents of the Guapi river have brought me any new lovers. There's been no time to think about anything erotic, and the only flirting came from Miller, a boy of around six who claims to have found three girlfriends among the visitors to his town, one of whom is me. However, I've come to understand that my form of resistance is intense love.

I'll tell you more about that another time. It will be a new excuse to write to you. Don't think I've forgotten the letters I owe you after Tumaco. I like owing you letters. It's a good excuse to remain, and resist, in this world of words, which, like the palenques established by fugitive slaves, is a place of freedom and escape.

Hugs,
    Veliamar

Dear friend,

Just as you love my stories, I love your short replies. Managing to say so much in so few words is a rare privilege.

You know how I used to love travelling around Antioquia for work. When you write to me from its towns, it brings back memories scented with good coffee.

I wasn't planning to go into detail just yet about my own way of resisting. But, I admit, you made me think. And now I realise some texts are more suited to being spoken aloud and in person, but I'll have a go at answering.

I'm like the Pacific Ocean, pressing at the river with its tides to make it flow the other way, or lapping at the land when its waters rise, when it feels like gaining inches of new ground. You need strong motivation to stick to this way of life, which isn't exactly a fight against the world, but rather the certainty of forging your own path.

My motivation, I now know, is intense love. The only way I can imagine doing this is with a boundless love for all that I've been making of myself. What gets me through is a great passion for how I read the universe, and for this place I've built for myself in the world.

I have a fierce love for my freedom, and for the people I love. What sustains me in my ideas is the deep love I feel for them and for the way I have built them. Loving like that is what helps me keep going here, what helps me resist. Loving like that is what gives me the strength to live like the tide, sometimes waning, but then returning with force. I dive in without any certainties, with only the peace and hope that love brings.

I wonder if we all resist in some way, if we all oppose some force acting on our lives, and refuse to give in, and build a place from which to fight back. Do we always have something to oppose, something to avoid and work against, or are there people who don't oppose anything, whose whole lives are spent floating with the current, with no force pushing them in the opposite direction to what they seem to want? You, for example: do you resist in any way?

I wonder, too, if it's true that it's boundless: is there a limit to that love? Is there a limit to my commitment to my chosen path, or to my certainty that this is my vocation? Maybe there is, and it could be the moment, or the place, where changes and desertions occur.

For now I feel a boundless love and I remember having felt it for some time.

Kisses,
　　Vel

Quibdó, 24 October 2016

Our bodies, my dear friend, are made for pleasure.

Last week, as I was swimming in Gorgona, looking through my snorkel at the ocean floor, my movements soft, I felt the seawater caressing my skin and basked in the pleasure of looking. And what a pleasure, too, to bite into the arazá fruit fresh from the tree. Tasting the bitterness in my mouth and then licking my lips, which were slightly swollen, tingling from the mix of sourness and salt.

Whenever I walk on the beach, I savour the pleasure of the sand between my toes. The sea breeze messes up my curly hair, so deliciously gently that I forget I'll end up with a huge great tangle on my head.

You must be very familiar with the pleasure of a good cup of coffee, the smell of it, the taste. Not to mention the pleasure we derive from good books. And melodies in our ears, like whale song under the sea, like whispers at intimate moments. Or the voices we invent as we read the words of someone who writes to us.

There's the pleasure of feeling our own body, and the emotions we can evoke when we're alone. Like last night, while I was reflecting on what I'd write to you about pleasure.

And there's the pleasure to be found in other bodies. A pleasure as yet undiscovered, because there's pleasure, too, in imagining the things we know will feel good.

Thinking about pleasure brings me back to resistance. I wonder if there might be a bit of a clash. Sometimes we resist and sometimes we don't; sometimes we let ourselves be overcome. I wonder again what makes me resist when I want to, and what sweeps all my resistance away. The answer, it seems, is always the same: love.

Veliamar

Quibdó, 21 November 2016

Dear friend,

I don't really understand my impulse to share these things with you, but here we are. You must have done something to earn this vote of trust. I've already told you about being a safe harbour.

I sometimes feel there's an old woman somewhere out in the universe, weaving my life with meticulous care. Each thread is carefully chosen: it seems she never misses a thing, never forgets my old desires, and likes to play at working in wonderful coincidences that bring a smile to my lips. I'm not sure if the end result is like a motete, or if it's closer to a mola tapestry because of all the colours, or if it's a multi-coloured motete.

Anyway, some years ago I met a man I liked, and in one of life's moments of daring I told him so at an event. But then we didn't see each other again. I also told a friend who happened to know him, and she pretty much said he was out of my league. My answer was simple: well, I like him and now he knows, and that's enough for me.

On Saturday, that man was in Quibdó, for the festival that takes place here now. I saw him in the afternoon, but barely remembered that I actually knew him. A distant smile and a 'Hi' from a few yards away were all I needed. But he decided to come over, and interrupted the conversation to greet me with a warm hug and ask a couple of questions about why I hadn't been in Medellín. I got as far as explaining that I live here now, and we parted ways with the usual promise of 'See you around'.

I'd have no problem admitting here in this letter if I'd desired him that afternoon, or if I'd carried on thinking about him. But the truth is that I didn't. A couple of hours later I was at the concert, waiting excitedly for the hottest new chirimía group to start.

At one point I saw him from afar and remembered I liked him. When I told the friend I was with, she reminded me that lots of girls liked him. My response: I don't mind being one of a crowd. In my mind the idea persisted that there was no chance of anything happening, so I settled for being just another person whose eye he'd caught.

A couple of hours later I ran into him again, and we said hi and promised to see each other soon. This time it was true. And then he reminded me about the last time we'd met and talked, almost five years ago. By that point, enough pipilongo, aguardiente, beer and viche had passed our lips that everything flowed along smoothly. However, there had been no great explosion inside me until that moment, not even from the couple of kisses while we were dancing very close together to songs that other people were dancing to fairly far apart.

Only in his hotel room, when he dived straight between my legs with his mouth and marked the first contact between our naked bodies, did I feel like I might explode from so many sensations at once.

He admired the mathematical proportions of my big bum and small breasts. He celebrated the contrast between my skin and his, and the softness as they rubbed together, over and over.

We were surprised – me as well as him – by how easily certain things happened which with other people are a whole time-consuming ritual. Many times, we wondered aloud if it was the effect of the pipilongo, and vowed to repeat this intense sex every time our paths crossed in the world. I think, for him, it was brought on by the fetish of being with a black woman in this earthly paradise. To be honest, I don't have much faith in the spirituality or emotional depth of many men. For me, I think it was the exultant sense of having been given the gift of what I wanted, even if I'd forgotten I wanted it.

The synchronicity of that encounter, its intensity and perfection, contrasted with the dissonance there still is in these events run by outsiders in our Chocoan town. We're getting a bit better at couple dancing now, we're beginning to understand what Quibdó wants and vice versa, but there's a long way to go before they fit together as seamlessly as my body and the body of this man who we can simply call an artist, whether because of his profession or because of the work he produced with my body in the early hours of that morning.

I don't believe in the promises of intense sex to come. I don't even know if we'll have another inter-esting conversation. All I could do was feel. All I could do was savour what was kindled inside me, in the hope that more than sex will be kindled in this city thanks to all these worthwhile projects.

Hugs and kisses,
 Vel

Dear friend,

I know my stories must at times carry with them my craziness, at others my musings on the world and every so often my sadness, or perhaps they show you how sane I can be.

I suppose one way of summing up a life could be describing the different phases we've had in our relationship with sex. Perhaps it's precisely because of the way sex can be so spiritual or so basic, something utterly raw or a profound meeting of souls. It can even be both things at once.

By this point in my sexual journey, which isn't all that wide-ranging but is something I've thought about a lot, I'm not sure it really is impossible to mix short-lived and total connections. In fact, that's the dynamic that seems healthiest to me, and which allows me the freedom to live without limiting myself and without feeling that I have unfinished business with my pleasure.

It's really magical what you're experiencing at the moment. It feeds the soul. There's a time for everything: you must have had, and will have again, times in your life when pleasure takes over and you remember it's not worth resisting.

I think what's given me stability is that mix of total and short-lived connections; it's having all my senses invested in a single life project, which, as I've told you before, I've so often discussed, examined and analysed with my husband, and from there, from that place which is also a safe harbour, sometimes allowing myself the pleasure of thinking only of my senses.

I hope you achieve your goal of seeking total connections and avoiding the short-lived ones. Being in a purely romantic phase is a beautiful thing. I could skip the stories of my sex life for a while so as not to put you off, or we could carry on talking about everything. After all, we don't need reminding that other people's stories can help us find paths through our own.

I feel flattered by your confession.

Kisses and hugs.

Grisela's eyes are like two black olives, smooth and very shiny. Her hair is curly and black, so black, as if it were made of fine strands of night. Her mother loves combing it and sometimes gives her little braids. Grisela's skin is dark and lustrous, softer than the skin of a panther playing in the rain. She's like the Niña Bonita in Ana María Machado's story, and on Sunday afternoon she listened attentively to that story when we read it together and compared the pictures in the Spanish and Portuguese-language editions.

Grisela has come to hear the stories on countless Sundays with her younger siblings, Ana Pastora and Hainover.

This Sunday, after we'd said goodbye and I was getting ready to leave, I went to wash my hands in a tank for collecting rainwater, and when I turned around, this niña bonita was running towards me, trembling and weeping uncontrollably. It was less than fifteen minutes since we'd said goodbye. When I saw her, I held out my arms and asked what had happened. Grisela flung herself at me and hugged me very tight, saying: 'They killed my brother.'

Her tears landed on my skirt, and mine collected on my chest. I didn't know what to do.

She asked me to help her unlock an old mobile phone of her mum's, then I went with her to her house, which is really a shack with a dirt floor and rickety walls made of planks of wood, where the cleanliness is at odds with the poverty.

I spoke to the children's mum for a bit, and she explained which child had been killed: a boy of eighteen who was working 'along the Iró river'. I talked to her about how intelligent her children are, and about the plan she'd had – which fortunately she's now given up on – of sending Grisela to live with her godmother.

Grisela gave me another hug, another which never seemed to end. She clung to my waist as tight as she could and more and more tears fell.

All I could think to do was leave them a little money, the small amount I usually carry with me there for safety reasons. And then I left, with the cries of 'Thank you, Seño!' echoing in my head.

Thanks for what? All I can offer are stories. And what's the point of reading stories when life is so hard?

This has left me very sad. I cried that afternoon. I'm crying now. I'm asking myself a lot of questions. I feel like what I do is worthwhile, but I don't know to what extent. The children wait for us, they run behind the bus when they see me through the window, they don't fight or tease each other while we're reading any more, and they answer my questions about the stories we read. I still vividly remember the first time, when I read with four girls, and now forty turn up, thirty-five at the very least.

People need so much and all I can offer is to sit on the floor together and read a story.

Thank you for being here so I can get this off my chest.

Lots of love.

Quibdó, 12 December 2016

H_{ey,}

The first week of December was the last session of the Pacific Diploma, and now we just have to hand in our texts for the final publication. I didn't tell you anything about the session in Buenaventura; nothing particularly out of the ordinary happened there. It was more important to talk to you about the lover in the days leading up to it.

I wanted to tell you that on Sunday I heard the good news that Grisela's brother wasn't killed after all. There was a mix-up. He came last week to visit his family, to tell them he was sorry for the misunderstanding but that as they could see he was alive and well. If only things were always like that.

This weekend was the end of the two children's clubs. I was very happy, and even shed a few tears. It feels incredible that this is really happening.

Did you know you're an important part of all this? Did you know you're an important part of my life?

My dear friend: like everyone else, I have a father. He's young – fifty-four years old – to have such a grown-up daughter. He's studied and worked hard. A self-made man, he did all he could to get an education and develop an impeccable CV: he's been the mayor of Bahía Solano and the government secretary and treasury secretary in the Department of Chocó, as well as managing the Chocó Liquor Company and heading up major production initiatives in the region. I've always admired him a lot for his career.

When I was born, my dad was twenty and studying for a degree in public administration in Bogotá. I stayed with his parents, my grandma Belisa (the person I love most in the world, from whom I inherited my character and a lot of my physical appearance) and my granddad Toñera (Manuel Antonio Vidal). My grandma was a baker and my granddad was a driver for the Technological University of Chocó.

Because of the situation, I don't think there was time for my dad to get used to the idea of having a daughter. My mum was even younger and still at school, so she came to Quibdó to study while I was with my grandparents.

My grandparents became my mum and dad, and their other nine children were my brothers and sisters. My grandparents' house in Bahía Solano was paradise.

The smell of bread, the custom of collecting eggs from the henhouse each morning, the afternoons on the beach playing with my uncles and aunts. What I didn't know was that all the while, I was growing apart from my biological parents.

Later on, once I was at university in Medellín, having spent several years in Quibdó and in Cali with my biological mother, and several more with my aunt Ludys (my mum's older sister, who became my second mother after my grandma, or perhaps my third, if I count the one who gave birth to me and loves me so much, whose name is Celia), I experienced a profound sadness, anxiety and insomnia, which led to, or rather explained, a very serious depression. I was taken to see a psychoanalyst, several psychologists and, for a long time, an excellent psychiatrist.

It was a difficult time, with plenty of tears and painful conversations – because our words had touched a nerve in my soul. The process always focuses a lot on a person's relationship with their parents, and my case was no exception.

I grew a lot. I learned. But most of all I tried to weave a new way of relating to my father that hurt as little as possible. My father has a very strong character and isn't always easy to get on with. There had come a time when I decided not to speak to him any longer because I found our conversations so painful. At twenty-two, I resolved not to accept any more financial help from him. Although that made my life very complicated in terms of supporting myself, because my mum had no way of giving me the money that my dad always had without fail, it took an emotional weight off my shoulders. From that point on, I got used to making things happen by myself. It was a lot of effort. I was always looking for work and although that meant all-nighters, early mornings and a gruelling schedule of classes, I felt strong and able to do it, and as I made progress with the things I wanted to achieve, I felt stronger and more capable still.

With my therapists' help I felt I was healing my wounds, and one day I decided to speak to my dad again. I approached it in a way that would allow me to have a healthy relationship with him, and that's how things have been ever since. It's a relationship I manage like a juggler: I know just what to say and what not to say, I never ask for anything, I never seek support. Depending on my dad's moods we might spend a nice afternoon together, or we might go a long time with no more than a 'Hi, how's it going?'

With my mother, it's different. She's a very sweet woman, and she also became a Christian some twenty years ago. We love each other and talk regularly, but we obviously keep a bit of distance; we don't have a big commitment to each other. Still, we're affectionate and try to spend a few days together each year.

My strongest family ties are with my grandmother Belisa, my uncles and aunts on both sides, and my cousins Yajaira and Idier, who are like a sister and brother to me, as are Elkin, Pacho, Willinton, Belisa and Diego, my parents' younger siblings. This has given me a broad network of affection, which also includes my thirty-eight other first cousins and my biological brother and sister, the children of my father.

One of my reasons, which weren't always fully conscious, for coming back to Chocó, was to be close, closer, to my family. I've always said it was to be close to my grandma, and I've managed that.

This proximity to my dad has made me more adept at managing my relationship with him. That's what I used to think, what I want to think. Only there are times, like now, when my heart gets tied up in knots.

My dad has a flat here in Quibdó, just five blocks from where I live. And he comes to the city fairly regularly. He arrives in Quibdó and doesn't send a message to tell me he's here. Twice now I've run into him in the street, and then I act surprised and happy. But both times I already knew he was here and that for some reason he'd chosen not to tell me. And then I swallow the pain and tell myself again that it doesn't matter. Now that I'm working on this project, which is so important to my life, and find myself down certain alleyways where I need some support, some encouragement, an alternative plan, a bit of money, it breaks my heart to know that I can't turn to my dad. Not because he isn't there, but because he wouldn't say yes.

Last weekend we ran into difficulties while we were out in my uncle's car. My uncle didn't answer when I phoned him. Then I phoned my dad, and his response was cold. It was clear he wasn't going to help. I quickly pretended I'd just wanted to see if he was in Bahía Solano and could go and find my uncle. He said he wasn't – he was in Quibdó. The same old story. He'd been here almost a week. It's New Year. But only for that reason, only because he wanted to make absolutely clear that he couldn't help, did he tell me he was in town. And I got no message afterwards checking how I was or if I'd solved the problem. Nothing.

This week my husband passed him in the street. A polite wave and that was it!

All those times, I found a solution. I usually do. I don't get stuck. I have my husband's unconditional support. And luckily I have plenty of friends here. Luckily I've learnt to always look for solutions, ever since I was very young. But there are days when my heart plays dirty tricks on me, or my head does; days when I'm more vulnerable and have to deal with the pain, and then I cry a lot, like now, while I'm writing to you.

After so many years working in politics in Chocó, fortunately without any trouble from the regulators – which is unusual here – my dad knows the city, knows the region and usually has numbers in his bank accounts that give him financial peace of mind. But most of the time I can't even ask him to have lunch with me; he chooses to make it that way by keeping his presence in the city from me.

Again, I don't know why I'm writing all this to you. Maybe I needed to write it. To get it off my chest. Maybe I needed to cry a little, or a lot. You don't know what you've got yourself into by opening this door. I feel calmer now. In a few minutes I'll probably have forgotten all this. Everything's sorting itself out.

There's been a lot of female power in my life. Sometimes I feel I've really missed that paternal affection, that male presence. I often remember my grandad. Everyone says he loved me more than anyone. I feel as if, in losing him, I lost my true father. That was many years ago now. But affection and pain aren't measured in years.

Hugs, my dear friend. Lots of hugs.

So you see, there's also a wounded Velia, full of tears. And one that gets up again quickly. Life demands it of me.

Veliamar

Quibdó, 15 January 2017

It's amazing to have taken the plunge and be spending my time on something I'm passionate about. However, a project doesn't become any less challenging just because it's something beautiful that fills your soul. Maybe the guarantee I have is that I'm going to keep on loving this, however big the challenge.

These days have been wonderful and far from easy. We've had support from lots of friends, we've felt the anxiety of being low on resources. Some ideas are beginning to materialise, but it's overwhelming not knowing how to put a price on certain things, or where to begin with others.

Doing the accounts, paying the accountant, planning the projects, talking to other organisations, managing my time, not letting go of the chances to read or write. Sometimes I get scared. Then I remember that the best decision I've ever made was coming to Chocó and being able to see the children smile when we get off the bus with a bag full of books.

I remember the mothers who come over and hug me in the street, or the little hands that high-five me from a passing moped after someone aboard shouts, 'See you, Seño Velia!'

I'm only writing to you to remind myself it's worthwhile. I'm only writing to you so I remember I have you, and can come here and write on difficult days, days when I feel afraid, when I worry we'll never get anywhere with these projects.

Send me a few words, the kind you know just how to say.

I think I'm eager for 21st January to come around so I can be reading stories to the children again. I'm also eager to get the better of a muddle in my head, or my heart. More about that soon.

Hugs,
Vel

My dear friend,

Last Sunday we were in El Futuro again. We now have ninety-four children signed up for the reading club, and we realised that about eighty of the local children had attended the club at least once. We hadn't been keeping an exact record, so it took us by surprise. It was very moving to see how the children's faces lit up when we arrived. The mothers told us they'd been asking about the dates: 'Is Seño Velia really coming back, Mum?' 'When's January 21st, Mum?'

Last Tuesday we held a sign-up session in the El Paraíso neighbourhood and ended up with twenty-eight kids. We'll begin there next Tuesday.

The day after tomorrow, Saturday, we open our new headquarters, Casa Motete. Tomorrow I'll send you some photos.

I have plenty of reasons to be happy. And I am. But my emotions are on hold, in a way. I'm not my usual bubbly, cheerful self. I'm not sure if it's something chemical – to do with the Graves' disease – or just a time of less effusiveness, of enjoying my happiness more calmly. I don't get paralysed; I keep going with each task. I feel the fullness of my soul because of everything that's coming.

I've had to face up to complicated things, like explaining to someone very dear to me that she couldn't become a 'partner' in Motete just by making a big donation, because it's a not-for-profit organisation and I can't promise personal benefits in return for funding. We ended up without her money but with the peace of mind that comes of sticking to our vision. 'But that doesn't work here in Chocó'; 'But even if you do it like that, no one here will believe you because no one here does it like that'; 'But here, a non-profit is just another business for hire'.

And I, with that lack of effusiveness which is turning into calm, and with my usual firmness, simply said no. That I can't accept money on the basis that it will lead to future benefits for whoever donates it. I don't intend to work every day for anything other than reading promotion and the aim of reaching more children. I'm not going to sign contracts to acquire financial support if that means granting special privileges to investors. All of us who work here have to have a salary and get by on that, but no more.

So on I go, dealing with the everyday challenges. And with each day I feel more encouraged by the idea that I've made the best decision. It's just that I'm more thoughtful now. Water still flows within me, but more gently. I'm no longer that wild sea, those crashing waves; I'm the bay when it's calm, deep, almost still.

Even my love affairs are on hold. I think it's something other than sadness – I don't feel sad. I think that as certain activities become part of your life, they become part of you, of your day-to-day existence, and they also stop catching you by surprise. You accept them more peacefully.

I take a deep breath, reflect, give thanks for all I'm receiving. I give thanks for what I have, like the chance to come and tell you these simple things.

Kisses.

Dear friend,

It's just sixty days since Casa Motete opened its doors. In sixty days we've begun our first programme of activities, we have seven children's reading clubs on the go, we've been visited by Maité Hontele and Teresita Gómez, we've run a workshop for teachers (Motete on the road), we've set up a teachers' club with twenty-three members and we've run workshops with children in eight different educational settings in Quibdó.

I've travelled twice as a guest to national events. We've opened this café every day and now we've bought a new café as well. There have been concerts, panel discussions and films, and we now hold a story time with regular visitors, from Monday to Friday.

Of the sixty days, I've cried on about twenty. Sometimes from joy, and many more from stress. I cry for a bit and then go back to work. On some days I've been exhausted, and on others I've been bursting with energy.

One of the most painful moments was the death of Brayan. He never missed a story time, and used to borrow books and take them home with him. He understood everything. At just nine years old, he could play the saxophone like a pro. Days earlier he'd asked me about the language in some of our books, and if I thought it was suitable for a child. We talked for a bit about the magic of books, how they can have anything in them and it's up to us to decide what to take and what to leave.

We read together one day, then the next day he didn't turn up and the day after that I left for a trip. I was in Bogotá when Roge called to say that something bad had happened to one of the local kids, the ones who came to story time. I flatly refused to listen. Annoyed, I told him not to pass on speculation, and to do me a favour and go to the house and ask what had happened. A few hours later he called back and said the child had died. Something genetic in his head, which there'd been no way of knowing about or preventing, took his life.

I cried uncontrollably. Everyone in Motete and the neighbourhood cried. Lili helped me think through what to do next. She suggested we do something at story time when I got back, just to heal our souls. And that's what we did. Every day we read a story that made us think about life and death, and about the pain and sadness we feel when other people leave us. Brayan's sister, cousins and friends were all in the group.

Without knowing it, we were weaving a strong bond with the community. The end of the week, the very day the last novena was said for Brayan, was also Brayan's birthday. That day we made a cake and invited the music teacher and his family, and we read, sang and celebrated Brayan's life.

There have been days when we've had plenty of money, and others when we haven't even had five thousand pesos to cover our costs. We have no electric fans, but we have chairs. We have no funds to buy books, but we got hold of a borrowed projector and now we read some stories from the Internet.

Never have so many things happened to me in so little time. I've never invested so much of myself, or received so much love for what I've done.

All this is very strange. It must be how things go when you board the right train for you. My dad, who, as you know, doesn't tend to give me presents, gave me some tickets to go to Bahía Solano for Semana Santa. I think that's when I'll slow down a bit and be able to see all this in perspective. I'll try to make out the hidden substance of it all, and then I'll come back and carry on with the programme, which is very wide-ranging.

Sixty nice days I felt like sharing with you.

Hugs, my dear friend,
    Vel

My dear,

I'm writing to you from Turbaco, in Bolívar. This time, life has gifted me the pleasure of spending three days with my mum.

It's been a hectic week, the kind you city people have. The list of good news stories for Motete is long. So is the list of things I've learned. It's very encouraging to compare ourselves to other organisations and see that we're on the right track.

I'm going to take part in some projects to train teachers and librarians with the Terpel Foundation and Fundalectura, and another with the SM Foundation, and we've begun a joint project with *Arcadia* for our new festival, FLECHO (Fiesta de Lectura y Escritura del Chocó), which will have the theme *Reading the Jungle*.

But there are three painful things I want to tell you, which have slipped in among the words and books:

1. Cote Lamus' *Diario del Alto San Juan y del Atrato* has finally been published. They did a good job, as always. I'm pleased, but I can't help feeling sad that an idea of mine, which I saw as an opportunity to raise funds for our activities, ended up being carried out by other people – people I trusted. In the end they just sent me a

note thanking me for submitting the text and asking for an address where they could send a copy that never arrived. They basically took the project away from me, even though what I'd asked for was a price estimate for publishing a certain number of copies that we could then sell, with permission from Cote Lamus' children, to raise funds. They hadn't even known about the text before that, but they fell in love with it and kept it.

2. The time has come to publish the end product of the diploma, the Satchel of Pacific Stories. But by the final stage, there was so much bad feeling that all the happiness I felt about my story being published had gone. They erased us completely: the invitation doesn't mention the writers, or include a photo of us. It says: 'Four weeks of creative immersion produced new stories from Afro-Colombian communities about the forests (jungles) of the Colombian Pacific.' As if the stories wrote themselves, and as if it were possible to be immersed in what you already are.

3. A love that never happened. I told you a while ago that I was keen to get the better of a muddle in my head, or my heart, I wasn't sure which. Well, I was talking about the beginning of a love affair, but I think it was further along in my imagination than it was in reality. Eventually the tangle in my head came undone, and it stayed in the category of a love affair that never was. It still hurts a little, I admit. But I don't know if the pain is because it never happened, or if it's awkwardness and anger because some of the love is still there, even

though nothing ever came of it. The problem is that I'm at risk of running into the object of this love face-to-face, and I don't know how I might feel.

Although I've reflected a lot on being married and at the same time letting myself feel the passions or interests that bring me life, I sometimes find myself worrying about the idea of being a woman who has eyes for no one but her husband. I wonder if it wouldn't be simpler to have my head in a single place, without the distractions that, although they have the charm of flirtation, sometimes lead to things like this awkward and even painful episode. But in the end I come back to the idea that this is my way of loving and perhaps it can't be changed.

I decided to write to the publisher and express my dissatisfaction about the book. I decided to write to my teachers from the diploma and tell them I'm annoyed about what happened in the final stage. Words help me work through my emotions. But in the case of the love affair, I think the words could be misunderstood and end up saying something I don't mean, or beginning an unnecessary chapter. So I don't have anything to write to that love interest. I can only write a little to you. And meanwhile I wait, hoping that when I see him face to face I'll find that the emotions really have been processed. Fingers crossed.

Lots of love,
    Vel

Buenaventura, 15 May 2017

I can see the sea from my window. It's calm, and the tide is high. I've never been afraid of the sea, not even on stormy days. At difficult times for the sea, I feel a kind of understanding, a certainty that it will pass, that it's only for a while.

I wish I could feel, now, amid everything that happens to me when I'm busy with work, that same calm the sea usually gives me. But this time it's not there. I'm scared. There's a lot to get done with Motete this week and we're never going to manage, and what's more we're on strike: the population has decided to take to the streets, and rightly so, to demand what has been denied us for centuries. We support the strike, and I can't wait to get back so I can join the marches myself, as I have done before, but under the circumstances we've had to close Casa Motete, which means a huge reduction in the chances of an economic miracle. I'm in Buenaventura, busy with something I'm sure will help us a lot, but which is keeping me away from Quibdó and leaving me with less time to work out what to do.

The fear makes me want to cry. I have a stomach ache. And in the end I don't cry or get sick with an upset stomach, I just carry on. I know we can make it through this and come out stronger, but it's like a huge wave, the kind that does scare me. It can't be a coincidence that I'm by the sea today, and able to look at it, contemplate it and find a little bit of peace.

Through the sea and these letters I want to find calm. Surely life is holding the solution to all the other problems just around the corner. It always has done before, and I hope this is no exception.

Quibdó, 26 May 2017

This is the story of a book and me. We met one Friday morning in my favourite place in the library: the children's section. It was love at first sight. And at first sight I also knew I had to give this book to my friend as a present. However, there was a long way to go between me meeting the book and the book meeting my friend.

I travelled to Bogotá, and once I'd found the money I was able to buy the book for my friend, but I couldn't post it. I brought it to Quibdó, and it was with me for a week. Then I took it to Cali, where I thought I was really going to post it, but then it turned out I had to save every last cent because in Cali I was broke. I didn't know when I'd be able to go back to Quibdó, so every peso made a difference.

Eventually I had to travel to Quibdó via Bogotá, and as a result it didn't make sense to spend the money on postage. That day was very painful. Under the most absurd circumstances they made me, and only me, get off the bus that was taking me to the plane and then, although some of my luggage travelled on, the book and I stayed put.

Simply You stayed there, keeping me company on that sad night. I read it again and decided to post it the very next day. Which I did: before setting off, I went to a post office and then the book and I parted ways.

I don't know what face my friend made when he received it: whether he smiled, whether he was pleased. I'd like to know if he liked it. But sometimes, a person receives a beautiful book full of love and doesn't say anything.

VeliAmar

Quibdó, 13 June 2017

These days are very hard to describe. It depends what lens you want to see them through. For you, I'll choose the lens I like the most: it's been a very creative time, we've had lots of ideas about how to make this dream grow, and we've received our first crowdfunding donation, which – what's more – was full of love.

Every day we've made sales in the café. Now we have a new partner for the reading clubs: a businessman who's donating water and juice. This morning two people came who want to film news segments about our work, one for Telepacífico and the other for Caracol y Bancolombia Más Cerca.

During this time, we've also learnt to be very patient and tried to pass that patience on to everyone else, including our creditors. We've had some lovely events, with lots of people and excellent performers. We've incorporated 'Pacific Acts' and 'Playtime' into our work sessions in the reading clubs. It's been so beautiful to hug, speak of the beautiful things we all have and explore our idea of what peace is.

It's very exciting to see all this happening, to get up each day and face the challenge of carrying on with this work I love so much.

Love to you too. And thank you,
Vel

Since your last birthday, you and I have exchanged some twenty-five different communications, each involving at least two messages – one there and one back. Over the course of the year, we've seen each other just once, and, aside from the day we met for breakfast, I think I've heard you just once more than that: when you sent me a voice note, probably because you were in a hurry. Geographically, we've been far apart more than ninety-five per cent of the time. However, you've always felt very close by.

I don't hear your voice, but something makes me feel that I have a part of you. I'm not quite sure what I mean by have, since I'm no great fan of possessives; it's more the sense that you're always near, and a strange certainty that I can count on you.

Times of crisis and my own bad manners make me behave selfishly. I'm always receiving encouragement, recommendations, support, and yet I keep forgetting to give them, or at least to give them to you. However, you must know that I'm also simply here. I don't know what for, but I am. And from within this dense jungle, and from the constant tragedy, the extreme humidity, the sight of sunset after sunset and the stories that save us, you can count on me. You have a part of me.

With love,
 Seño Velia

My body demands more hours of sleep, and a little more rest. The flat where I sleep – I'm not here at all during the day – demands more tidying, more cleaning, more of my time. My husband demands sex. Now and then an old lover demands flirting.

And I, as if I exist outside my own body, answer only the demands of Motete – of the performers, children and teachers that Motete brings together.

And from my friends I demand attention, support and affection, in the service of the only demands I respond to, which aren't those of the flat, or those of my husband, or those of old lovers.

I spend my time demanding your attention. It's encouraging when you say that passions demand everything from a person.

Quibdó, 17 July 2017

It's raining hard, as if the sky had forgotten it's meant to stop every so often, that there are days when it doesn't need to rain. It's rained all month, some days more and some less, but every single day. You learn to love the rain so much, and live with it for so long, that it stops being an excuse not to do things and becomes a part of life. And we talk about the appearance and heaviness of yesterday's rain, and today's, and we can't wait to find out how tomorrow's will be, as if it were an array of beautiful sunsets.

Which is why I'm here, despite the rain, trying to get up to date with my life. I went to bed early last night, and now I've set up a workspace in my flat and I'm ready to experience my first Monday off since we opened Casa Motete. It won't be a full day off because I need to go in this afternoon and do a few quick things, but I have everything I need here to write, read, and use the change of place and activity as a kind of rest.

I read some more of a little book I should have finished two weeks ago, and which I finally managed to finish today, and last night I came across a quote from Edward Morgan Forster which makes everything that's happening to me feel very meaningful. At the end of the day, he says, it all depends on words: 'words, the wine of life.' That must be why taking a break, for me, means having the time to sit here writing words, and encountering words that are yet to be read, and the really lucky thing is that my work involves playing at words with the children, wondering what more I can do to make other people fall in love with words as well.

I told you about our big achievement on Friday. It was the first time we made a million pesos' worth of sales in a single night. On Saturday things carried on really well. We saw the children from the reading clubs again, with some differences: we've now planned out the whole learning offer for the term, and we're involving the parents more, and we have the tools to set a baseline we can use to measure the development of the children's competencies.

In the neighbourhoods of El Futuro and Ciudadela MIA, we also made adjustments to involve the families more. It's a huge challenge, because in the most vulnerable areas there's less family participation: the children are like little autonomous beings who go around the place getting involved in all sorts of things, in any activity that's on offer, sometimes without their parents even knowing. Still, we'll keep trying. We've explained to each parent or older sibling what we're doing, and that it's a two-year process and their participation is important.

We're still organising our finances. It hasn't been easy, but we're managing to get rid of the deficit, and I think that, at the rate we're going, we'll end the year in good financial shape. That means something like breaking even with zero debt, rather than any big profits, but I think that's a major achievement considering the time Casa Motete has been open.

Although we're on top of the rent now, it was a worrying situation and it's got me thinking a lot about the building we use as our base. It's scary that we can't rely on it long-term. It feels important to think creatively here: what can we do to reduce the risk? This is like our homework at the moment. I wasn't planning to consider it now, but it looks like we need to.

Many of the things that happen with Motete weren't really part of my plans, but it seems to have a schedule and a life of its own.

I'm sending you a big hug, wishing you a happy week and reminding you that it makes me very happy to know you're there, looking out for me.

Vel

My dear friend,

Everything here is getting better and better. Balancing work and time off is becoming a habit and Motete's activities are beginning to feel routine, by which I don't mean they're boring but that they're a part of life. And I like all that.

Even the good news and intensive efforts at different times in the month feel like part of normal day-to-day life now, though we haven't stopped finding that exciting and surprising. And in the end, that surprise and that joy also form part of our daily life.

Last Saturday, the mother of Andrea, who I greeted very happily on her return to the reading club, asked me how I always managed to be like this, so happy, and so loving with the children.

It's very beautiful that it doesn't take any effort at all, and that it's 'always' like this.

So, as I imagine happens when children grow up, Motete is leaving me time once again for the things I love and enjoy, but couldn't concentrate on fully in previous months. The long hours spent doing nothing but reading, whole mornings spent plotting out the shape of a text, the feverish search for a particular poem, writing to you about life: all the things that, together with the work of reading promotion and running this cultural project, are what happiness is.

I'm working on a writing project that I hope to bring you when I come. Which won't be on the 3rd any more, but one or two weeks later. I'll let you know. Then I'll be back here again with my long letters and my stories: on Saturday, when I read a José Manuel Arango poem with the children and talked about Porfirio Barba Jacob, I remembered the importance of poetry in my life. It's like bathing in beauty or drinking the awareness of life in a single gulp; it's what it means to exist and, in the midst of it all, to submerge yourself in a tiny space that can reveal everything. It brings with it nostalgia, pain, happiness, many possible emotions. When I read a poem, it's like taking a deep breath and the air bringing with it the feeling described by the poem.

I remembered, too, that my life is full of poetry thanks to the sea, the Chocó sunsets, the water that falls from the sky and flows over the land, and this beautiful habit of writing to you and waiting for a reply.

And no one can live without poetry.

Veliamar

Dear friend,

As if Motete weren't enough, and as if everything here were ready and in place, I've begun collaborating with the women from the Gender Commission of the COCOMACIA, the greater community council of the Atrato river. It's made up of 124 community councils in Antioquia and Chocó, and has one of the country's biggest collective territories of black communities.

The seven women who make up the gender commission are brave. I could tell from the moment I saw them. They show what it means to empower women in rural communities. Thanks to their work, which has covered this collective territory from river to river, district to district, women now have posts on the management committee and serve as representatives of several local councils.

Yesterday afternoon, as we sat with the sun beating down on their office, we got to know each other better and I learnt that they're trained to smile in the face of adversity. It's two years since they've had a project that's enabled them to make any money, but they still go out to the communities each week. They still organise marches, occupations, workshops; they still come on foot from their homes and then walk on together for the dignity of women. They have a restaurant and a handicraft workshop, but they're both closed due to lack of capital, lack of support, and a few other things.

So I've committed to working with them, to giving them what I have and joining forces to get hold of what we don't have. I've got no idea what's going to happen with all this. So far, I have a very good architect who's going to redesign their spaces, and a friend who's included them in a six-month project that will help them generate some income. I have my strengths, my freedom and the conviction that backing their dreams takes nothing away from my own.

This evening, as I watched the sun set behind the jungle on the other side of the Atrato, I thought about how it all comes down to sowing seeds of hope. What you do, what I do, is read aloud to other people the story that encourages us every day, the story that says that just a bit further on, round the corner from that decision or that extra bit of effort, written on the page of a book, in the scent of some saplings or the taste of a plate of food, is the life we have always dreamed of.

Medellín, 15 September 2017

Of all the coffees, breakfasts and other times we've met up, yesterday's was my favourite. I could feel the freedom and trust we've built out of words.

These letters back and forth, with our hearts open (mine more so than yours), make me feel you close by, familiar; I feel known by you and free to exist.

The coincidence of us both thinking about publishing all these letters in some form, the joke about how well-behaved my hair was, the spontaneous response to my complaint that you haven't been to Chocó. The feeling of peace that comes of having enough time. We didn't find it wanting because we know there will be more.

I liked seeing you. I liked the way you are. I liked that we watched the sunset together.

That night I met up with Amalia Lú. She's giving a talk at Motete on September 30th, and that day's 'motete' (the money people put in the basket) will go to us. She's also going to donate some books for us to sell that day and in the future. And other things too: it was definitely a very productive meeting.

Then we went to a dive bar on the corner of Palacé and Bolivia, which is where the trans prostitutes hang out. Outside, the sense of danger, of a place that's off limits for the 'respectable' people of the city. Inside, a little bar full of charm, and love, and people who know each other, people who feel at home, and request the songs they want, and dance, and feel safe despite being in a place that seems dangerous, because people feel safe where there's trust.

We had a brilliant time. It was a beautiful night in a Medellín that felt different to the one I used to live in. At half past two I dropped Amalia Lú at her hotel and then carried on to mine.

Medellín, 6 October 2017

These days have been very intense. During the San Pacho fiestas, which are the traditional local celebrations in Quibdó, and famous for being very long, there were events at Motete every day. Lots of partying, lots of drinking of viche moonshine and pipilongo. And now here I am. I've had a lot of fun, and I've learned a lot.

Sometimes everything happens very quickly and I feel like there's no time to think. It cuts into my writing time, too. How to slow down? I'm managing to persuade myself that Motete has its own rhythm. I want to make space for some calmer moments. Find a way of settling things down. I want more roots.

When I don't have so many stories to tell you about myself, and all my stories are about Motete, I wonder about the balance between this thing which is so much a part of me and my own self.

I'm surprised by my newfound ability to set aside things that seem to be so personal. Or rather, perhaps, by how personal and intimate this project is.

I'm leaving tomorrow, this time without a date for returning to Medellín. Once again, without knowing when I'll see you next. That would upset other people, but it gives me a pleasure like fireflies' light, an enjoyable flickering, a glow that doesn't dazzle. Nothing like the glare of lightning bolts. The magic of a constant glimmer, even if it's not always visible.

It occurs to me that our feeling for each other is like the tide: we're always there, sometimes closer – high tide – and sometimes further away – low tide – but always present. And when we see each other, we're like fireflies. All flickering, magical, necessary for life.

We'll stay here, then, and see each other when the time is right.

Kisses,
　Vel

Quibdó, 17 October 2017

This afternoon, when I left the El Paraíso reading club, in which we wrote down our biggest secrets and fed them to the fire – the children wanted to burn them to make them disappear – there was a torrential downpour, heavier than usual, so much so that a lightning bolt damaged the runway at the airport.

I stayed in the local church, where I'd just had a meeting; outside, a woman of twenty-seven was sheltering on the pavement with her one month and seventeen day-old baby and her three-year-old son. I invited her in, to a space which isn't mine by property, or proximity, or religious belief, but I couldn't leave her out there. After a while, curiosity drew us back to the door. The woman's husband, older daughter and stepson had arrived. She introduced them to me and when I said hello, the girl said we already knew each other. That I was the woman from the Bank of the Republic. I greeted her with the affection that these moments bring about, and right away she said, almost imitating my voice: 'Rosa's Bus'.

I hugged her tight. *Rosa's Bus* was the story I'd read the day we met in the play area at the bank. It talks about Rosa Parks, the woman on the bus: the black woman who wouldn't give up her seat to a white man, which led to the boycott that ended up overturning segregation laws on public buses.

It was an epiphany, as if in that moment I suddenly saw all the effects a well-chosen story can have, a story read with love, a story that has everything to do with a person. We read it in May, more or less, and there it is, intact in her head, making her feel more things than I can imagine: that she's like Rosa, that she can do stuff, that it's worth fighting for something... I don't know, so many things. And next to the image of that book, Seño Velia's face. Such a responsibility!

Then I remembered I was meant to share some stories with you that I wrote last week, all in one go, over two days. They came to me just like that, like an epiphany. They're about moments when teenagers or young people discover themselves. What inspired these stories was meeting Winner, a boy who came to perform at Motete with his dance group. I said hi, we introduced ourselves and I realised he didn't know what Winner meant in English. It was a surprise for him, and for his friends, the girls in his dance group.

Then the other stories began to come, partly from teenage memories, partly from anecdotes I've heard from my girlfriends and a couple from conversations with you. Let's see if you can tell which ones they are.

A huge hug.

Quibdó, 26 November 2017

I have a lot of tasks to get through; so many that I feel sick. I call it anxiety sickness. I want to do everything, and I'm sure doing everything will bring me peace of mind. But I find it impossible to begin, and decide to write to you instead. Then I put off the act of writing to you – I don't have time – and with that I put off the possibility of making a start on the tasks.

Now here I am, trying out a new way of writing a to-do list, looking for motivation. And this place, which has been a rest stop, a confessional, a notebook, a travel journal and a harbour, will also be a driving force.

I tend to see every November 5th as the beginning of a new phase and the end of an old one. I realise it's only an illusion. But that makes sense: we're made of illusions.

Now that this thirty-sixth year has begun, the days have brought beautiful things. I've moved house and feel like I have a home again. The house I now live in has three floors. The ground floor will be the kitchen and storeroom for Motete. That's where we'll make the cakes, sauces and snacks, and prepare the meat. To clear a bit of space in Casa Motete, since it's really very small. And the first and second floors are Seño Velia's house. I've already chosen the plants that will go in my new garden.

I'll have a garden again. I have a bedroom whose big window, which lets in plenty of light, is adorned with the guanabana tree in the central courtyard. A beautiful piece of happiness. The house also seems to be in one of the few quiet parts of Quibdó. I'm happy there, and now I feel confident enough to hand in the adoption forms to Family Welfare. For a while my heart's been ready, but I've needed a space where I felt comfortable. I also feel I have a direction now, which I think is most important of all. Should I apply to adopt one child, or two, or three? I don't know. Maybe the answer will come as I'm filling in the form. We'll see what happens with that.

Last week marked a year since I last had a lover. Or, to be more precise, a sexual encounter with someone other than my husband. I don't see it as an achievement. For all that I sometimes toy with the idea that this year I really will come to my senses, it's never been a definite aim, and nor do I think it's about losing my senses. However, I have to admit that I feel quite proud, quite satisfied, even smug, which seems silly, but that's how I feel. Things are pretty good with my husband. I often remember one of these conversations, where you talked about a kind of more spiritual – or something like that – dimension of sex. I'm not sure if I'm quite there yet, but at least I'm in a place of reinventing it in order to enjoy it, after so many years together. Until now, I've sought out freshness or variety elsewhere, and it's worked, but now I'm looking within. It's more complex, more demanding, and that also makes it more beautiful, more satisfying.

I'm doing the Masters in Reading Promotion and Children's Literature. I'm giving it less time than I'd like – I could spend whole days studying the materials set by the teachers. I've never been so happy with an academic programme; every line I read feels valuable to me, and necessary for my work. I'm planning every detail of the stay in Spain next year. This work makes me very happy.

My father has decided to run to be a candidate for election, and strangely enough he called to ask my opinion on the comms management for an eventual campaign. I've thought a lot about how this love which I've found so painful is still so important in my life, and how every time he shows me his best side I react like a trusty dog, wagging my tail in excitement again. My heart doesn't give me a choice. My father's decision puts me in a particularly complex position, and given the visibility I now have, it will be a challenge to work out how to navigate it. I'll do my best to find a balance between Motete's independence and my family commitments. Luckily we've been establishing a place for ourselves, separately to my family name and based on recognition of our own efforts and work.

Motete's going well, with the usual challenges, the usual complications and plenty of opportunities, but I don't want to talk about that now. As I said before, I have a lot of tasks to get through. It's almost too much for me. Neither my body nor my mind can handle all these obligations, but I have to do what I always do, take them a few at a time, one at a time, like the tides, at a pace that ebbs and flows.

María Osorio, the owner and editor of Babel, asked me to send her my writing. I'm scared. It's something else on my to-do list. I need to do it.

Reading back over what I've written here, I like this life a lot. It has plenty of flaws, and there's a lot still to build, but I like the way it's going.

I might disappear a little, but I have no intention of getting lost.

Hugs,
Vel

Quibdó, 14 January 2018

A year after first starting work on this building, I finally feel like it's the way I dreamed. It's a collection of warm, special spaces. A collection of welcoming details. With books all around, neatly arranged. Everything has its place. It's like a single area and at the same time it's like a cultural centre with various sections. That makes me very happy. Last year we managed to pay off a lot of our debts, much more than we were expecting towards the end.

Motete, now, is like a baby learning to walk. On February 3rd we'll be one year old, and I'd say it's a healthy baby. There's a long way to go, but it has a bright future. There's a clarity to what we're doing, and although that could change, it means our work is focused.

I'm enjoying my course and got a good mark for my first assignment.

The Ministry of Municipal Education got in touch because they want to collaborate with us. The fear hasn't gone, the risks haven't gone, and nor have the days when we're low on funds and it seems like there's no solution. There are still days when no one turns up, because the city still prefers to drink and show off in the bars and clubs, in the luxury establishments built with cash of dubious origin. And when that happens, I make a delicious coffee, cut a slice of musa paradisiaca plantain cake and sit down to savour it in a corner of Casa Motete, while I read one of the thousands of poems that live in this house.

I couldn't go to Bahía Solano for New Year. I always miss it, but now I feel a fullness that reminds me of the sea. An immense fullness. And that fullness drowns my fears.

In a very fluid way, without putting up a fight, I've turned my back on flirting, and changed the conversations I have with friends who were once lovers. I no longer feel at all attracted to men who aren't my husband. And I know it seems like I'm only saying this as a strategy to please you, but there's no need to lie or invent masks here by now. What seems to be going on is that every part of my life is full. Motete is like a lover demanding all my attention, and I'm comfortable with that. Words in the form of stories or nursery rhymes haven't yet come to me this year. But I know they will, and plenty of them. By now I'm used to the way everything here comes at the right time.

There are things about this city I find difficult; social dynamics that make me ask a lot of questions. I notice the way some people in the social and cultural sector are determined to get ahead whatever it takes. I also see the formation of black elites, or Quibdó elites, which appear to divide this already divided city even further. I've had to find my own style in my relationships here, and in the place this organisation is finding for itself. I can't bear being very visible; I can't bear the idea of becoming what people here call an icon. I don't want to be the leader of anything. But I know that much of what I do inevitably sends me towards some of those things. I want this year, in which we're going to grow as an organisation, to be an opportunity to find a healthy and comfortable position for myself. I want it to be Motete and not Velia Vidal. I just want to keep being Seño Velia.

We'll face a lot of challenges this year, and our costs will be high as well. But after making it through year one, I'm almost certain we'll manage everything.

I want to keep counting on you this year, and I hope to see you again. I don't know when, or how, because I have no plans to visit Medellín. But life always sorts something out. Maybe this time, instead of watching a sunset in Medellín, we'll watch one in Quibdó.

Big hug,
    Vel

Quibdó, 25 January 2018

We've invented a world made of words for ourselves, a love made of words, of the desire for words, the prospect of words, the feelings stemming from words, from those already spoken and those yet to be spoken, and even those that will remain unspoken but that we know are there.

We don't write by hand. We don't go to the post office to seal an envelope and send it. Instead we use this medium, which is as instant as online chat, but much closer to a letter.

The letters I write are carriers of my soul, and I've grown used to your replies: dependable, essential, brief and precise. I don't feel like I need any more words in your replies: they never seem incomplete. Perhaps because I don't build them up in my head, or perhaps because I already know they'll be brief. Whatever the reason, they're enough for me.

I've never wondered if you write many letters, if you have other correspondences like the one that takes place in this world we've made. I haven't wondered if there are places where your words come pouring out.

In recent days, after reading a document you'd written, my own letters began to seem very trivial. It was overwhelming to see so many of your words right there, displayed to the world, delighting so many readers, and I felt jealous of those words that dance and glitter, jealous that they don't show off for my words. It's not about the recipients, and it's not about the many other letters: it's strictly about the words.

I imagined encountering you with a huge sack of words, pulling out great gleaming handfuls and flinging them into the air for everyone around, and then sometimes, slowly and carefully, you'd take just a few words from that enormous sack and offer them in response to my own vast, translucent and ever-visible sack full of words that are trying to shine. I want to believe that the words you give in answer to mine come from a secret pocket in that huge sack of yours, and that perhaps they're weightier words, special and carefully chosen. But I also realise this is how jealous people console themselves.

It probably goes without saying, but never mind. In a world of caresses, there will be jealousy over the caresses not given, or given elsewhere, to other bodies. In some places jealousy will be sparked by a glance, but here it's jealousy over words.

I can't explain it any better. It's just a feeling I had. And my feelings aren't my fault.

Kisses.

My very dear friend,

It's not that I'm an expert at managing other resources. Maybe it's because I've got used to the absence of some, like money, and the abundance of others, like love, words or the waters of Chocó. But with time (the resource) I find I don't know how to manage it, and can't even work out how much I have available. It's not a question of hours or minutes. Watches make me uncomfortable. I've never felt anxious about the passing of days, except because of other people's demands. It doesn't upset me to get older, it doesn't scare me how quickly the months go by. The way I see it, things will happen come what may, so what difference does it make if they happen sooner than expected? I even find it easier to long for time to pass.

The thing is, Motete has grown and now not even several days put together would be enough for everything that needs doing. I have it all in my head, I'm not panicking and I know it's within our capabilities. But there's a lot that depends on me – on me finding the time to sit down and produce, and read, and write.

I carry on calmly, I don't have stress pains, I'm very careful about exercising and that makes me feel even better, but there's a set of things I just haven't been able to get done: plans, projects, documents, some reports, things that take concentration and a little peace and quiet.

How do you manage?

Quibdó, 12 February 2018

I have a strange sensation.

You must have heard that the ELN guerrillas have declared an armed strike in Chocó. From time to time they like to show how powerful they are and spread terror. Because of the armed strike, the organisations that work here have decided to remove their employees. 'Recall them', is the expression they use. Others have temporarily cancelled all trips here, 'for safety reasons'.

I completely understand. I think it's the right thing to do. However, I have to admit that I sense the separation on my skin, an abandonment of sorts. The worse everything gets, the more alone we are. It's as if some lives are worth more than others. The ones that are worth the most deserve to be protected, and are taken to safety, and prevented from coming to places that might put them at risk. But we don't have anywhere else to go. We stay here, left to our fate.

We've also had to do something similar. This weekend we couldn't go to the reading clubs in El Futuro, La Platina and Ciudadela MIA. It was very painful. But you have to drive on the main roads to get there. The saddest part is that what I feel in relation to people from international organisations or public institutions, the children will feel, in a way, in relation to us. To a very different extent, of course. Motete is still open, and we're not far away. But there are some things you just can't change.

We carry on, determined, convinced of the importance of being here. Trying to feel that being together is enough.

Your hug reached me and I'm sending another one back.
Vel

Quibdó, 22 March 2018

I want to send you my speech from the opening of our first Chocó Festival of Reading and Writing, or FLECHO. You witnessed everything. You helped me to make it possible, as always, so you deserve these words:

> Today I feel I hold the power of words in my hands, the power to use them at a strategic moment and leave a mark, and to allow myself, by using them, to rise to this occasion and ensure they're not among the words swept away by the wind. And so I will faithfully follow our inspiration, Federico García Lorca, who even today allows us to discuss what he said so many years ago, simply because he wrote it down.
>
> I'm writing these words, then, for the official opening of the Fiesta de la Lectura y Escritura de Chocó – our FLECHO – with the firm intention of reading them aloud so they can be heard and then read by others and for others, thereby forming this precious circle of words, in which we Chocoans already have the advantage because of our oral culture, and which is completed by this act of writing the words down to make them last. Writing with no thought for being published, with no dreams of

making money: just writing, almost as a natural consequence of reading, and then thinking, and then expressing what our desire dictates.

Writing, what's more, with the suspicion, so often confirmed, that in doing so from our place in the world we offer a unique perspective, one that's only possible here, where the Pacific and the Caribbean meet and receive the waters of three great rivers that begin small and then gradually widen, joined by thousands of tributaries, which are the love that makes them grow.

It's a perspective that could only ever come from Chocó, this great jungle between two seas. One of the most biodiverse corners of the world, which finished off its beauty with a huge historic mistake: slavery, a mistake we find painful and condemn, but which, in the long run, has allowed us to complete the circle of biodiversity and given this place, already so rich in nature, the good fortune to be inhabited not solely by indigenous people, but also by mixed-race mestizos and direct descendants of Africa. All three, on coming together here, in this land of water and rain, seas and humidity, were fertilised and gave rise to a particular culture: the culture of Chocó.

It's often said that we Chocoans 'are the Pacific', that we're 'Africa in Colombia', and there's some truth to both these expressions. However, they also reduce us, because that's not all we are.

Chocó is the Caribbean, Chocó is indigenous Colombia, and, as our Embera brothers and sisters rightly say, it is also Eyábida (of the mountain), Dóbida (of the river) and Phusábida (of the sea). And with each little part of what we are, we form a melting pot where culture no longer has limits and instead simply exists.

I'll give the example of 'motete', the word that blesses our organisation, where this FLECHO came into being. The word 'motete' is as much indigenous and European as African. It's a Caribbean and Pacific word, with an exact equivalent in Embera, and it's commonly used by Afro-Colombians and mestizos. So who could we say it belongs to?

That's how this land comes together, this land which leaves us no choice but to love it and tell stories about it.

When it comes to loving it, I'd like to quote the words of Eduardo Cote Lamus, from the department of Santander, who, like so many others, fell in love:

I began to love Chocó as a boy, while drawing a map of Colombia. The pencil would make its way up from the Ecuadorian border in the south and trace the edge of the sea, gather the mouths of the rivers, draw in the coves, the open-petalled rose of the San Juan and Baudó river deltas and the bays of Catripe, Cuevita, Birudó, before stealing space from the Pacific to mark out Cape Corrientes, topped with Arusí Point, where the Cugucho mountains end; I'd then bring my pencil back down and draw islands, low hills, the outstretched thumb that begins in Bahía de Utría and ends in Bahía Solano, after the circle called Nuquí, and then carries on up the coast to Panama. Once the map was finished I began on the rivers; at the bottom, the San Juan and the Baudó, and further up, the Atrato and its hundreds of tributaries; then the few mountain ranges and the faraway towns

with names that almost always end in -dó. Then I'd
draw in two boats to show where the sea was: a big
one in the Pacific and a smaller one in the Gulf of
Urabá. Since I wasn't short of imagination, I drew
the meeting of the oceans in the Truandó Pass. When
the map was ready, I looked at it from a distance and
thought it looked like a girl. And I thought that the
rivers, with their mellifluous names, couldn't possibly
be real.

As for telling stories about it, I could
mention my dear Amalia Lú Posso Figueroa, our
Arnaldo Palacios, my fellow Bahía Solano-born
Óscar Collazos or the great Rogerio Velázquez,
Zully Murillo, Jairo Varela or his mother Teresa
Martínez, or our Da Vinci, Alfonso 'The Wizard'
Córdoba, or Manuel Moya or his indigenous
elders who, like our black grandparents, find
that stories of the jungle are the best way of
teaching, and Waosolo or Murcy with their
photos. And the cooks, and the sculptures made
by our artists who work wood into Jaibaná
figures, Oquendo whales, Nazarenes, drums
and champa canoes; and the houses on stilts
that sometimes look out to sea, sometimes look
at the rivers and sometimes turn their backs,
telling us, through all that, the story of their
people, which is then painted by the maestro
Hoyos.

I could mention the singers of alabados at
vigils or the composers of lullabies for their
children, or outsiders – like me. The choruses
that grandmothers make up for each grand-
child, the songs sung or whistled by sawyers,
rice growers or fishermen as they work, and
the stories that, like ink in the muggy air, seem

to dissolve in the diary of a young girl; and I could mention, too, the thousands of verses that have been sung to the rhythm of 'Cocorobé'.

Chocoan culture is made of stories. Tales that are woven, tales that weave us. Overlain and knotted again and again, like catanga fishing baskets, and like motetes.

All the time, we're reading this jungle. Each one of those writers reads it, runs it over their skin, over their ancestors, over their own life experience and a new story is born. The jungle's story is told again and that story is stamped, written, sung and cooked, for the rest of us to look at, listen to, taste. And so we come together again and again around these multiple readings of our jungle.

The conflict has hit us hard in Chocó – all the different kinds of violence, all the groups who have established a presence in our territory – and the effects of this are well known. But maybe one of the most powerful and least discussed effects is the way it keeps us from gathering around the stories that make us.

Dark evenings spent listening to our grandparents' tales by the light of an oil lamp, young people clustered on street corners laughing at the top of their lungs, night walks through the woods just to reach a dance or a vigil – which are the same thing – or long hours collecting piangua oysters with women friends and neighbours, or going crabbing with a machete when the tide goes out at midnight, or hunting in the forest for weeks on end. Fishing expeditions with friends, trips to the sea and the rivers, games of bingo or dominoes, lots of bailes de pellejo with animal-skin instruments, and even traditional river processions, have been lost. Some sugar mills are no longer in use and hundreds of ovens have gone out.

Our exclusion from the racist, centralised Colombia that turns its back on Chocó made our stories into something unimportant. We rarely see ourselves reflected in books, films or television, and when we do it's usually an outside perspective full of stereotypes that reduce us or restrict us to a single version of ourselves. At most, we're the object of research by anthropologists who study us and then tell our story.

Music is perhaps the most significant form our stories have taken. However, it's important to add that this has led to us being pigeonholed in oral culture, which is seen as ephemeral and inferior, though nobody denies its beauty. Formal writing in Spanish is recognised and imposed as what's serious and important, in an attempt to legitimise or hide the inability to read other texts. Only through ignorance of the Embera, the Wounaan, or other Afro-Colombian narratives, would people choose the path of making them invisible.

So it is necessary for us to come together again, to recognise and value our own and others' stories, to return to the everyday act of gathering around words, discussing the various readings of our environment and approaching the world as who we are, which is, without doubt, an act of reconciliation. This is why we run FLECHO: so that these encounters can take place and allow us to build solid bridges towards peace.

And in the process we take up the challenge of organising our own literary event. We embark on the adventure of showing ourselves off, of making the news because of our potential and not our needs. We dare to revitalise the economy of our capital city by exercising our right to culture. We harness our communal, collective spirit to realise this joint project, with very little input from the fragile public institutions in our territory, but convinced that this path is also possible.

Let us tell, then, and write, over these five days, a new story that contains the deepest essence of Chocó: a story both oral and written, in poetry and prose, which allows us to read the jungle between two seas.

Dear friend,

Last week I felt ill, with various symptoms. I've been without my glasses for a while now and I think it's making me dizzy. I have a huge to-do list, and I never stop working. Happily, cheerfully. On the outside I'm always strong. I keep calm, try to find a solution for everything. I smile. I get up early and carry on.

I don't have time for anything besides Motete. What little time I do have is spent with my husband and at home, which is basically the same thing.

I'm very careful about what I say, which means I don't complain about all this to anyone. The few problems I talk about or mention are Motete's, which are nothing unusual, and I always end up saying we'll work something out. I've got used to talking about beauty: the beauty of achievements, of projects. However, it really does make me ill, and tired.

No doubt we'll talk about all this. No doubt it'll pass. What worries me most is the idea that I might be trying to hide my vulnerability, that I've decided it's my duty to be strong. And I forget I also have the right to collapse now and then.

I've written this, for example, at different moments, because every time I have to go and deal with something I put on a smile as usual, roll up my sleeves and get on with whatever it is.

What will happen if I let myself fall apart, if I stop pretending I'm strong, and scream and cry? What if one morning I decide I don't want to get out of bed?

That will probably come about before too long, as it has done before. Meanwhile, I carry on in this role.

Kisses,
     Vel

Sometimes I feel these letters have less poetry in them now, that they've become functional and nothing more. And that makes me a bit sad. I think perhaps it's because my life has less poetry in it, even though it's dedicated to poetry – in the sense of contemplating and then condensing what you feel into precisely the right words. I spend my time solving problems and dealing with day-to-day issues, and not contemplating very much.

Motete is growing. And it reminds me of the twelve-year-old Velia, who was so different, so easily upset, not very sociable at school, a loner at breaktimes, and who hadn't got used to her new dimensions: she was too skinny and had grown very quickly, so that she was too tall for how skinny she was.

I kept outgrowing my shoes, and since I'd had my first period, my aunts insisted I stop wearing the boy's shorts I liked so much. My cousin Yaja began to develop curves. She was very pretty, whereas I had no breasts or hips. I just went on getting taller, and my two front teeth stuck out more and more. All my top teeth, in fact.

So every day became a struggle to get to grips with my new dimensions. And meanwhile, I broke every glass object in my path. I was always tripping and falling over. A couple of times I fell in class and got mercilessly teased. At home I felt safe, or safer, though it was also quite awkward: since it was my aunt's house and not completely mine, it was embarrassing to keep breaking things. But out and about, I didn't feel good at all.

I'd only been in Cali a few months and it was a very difficult time: a new school where I was singled out because I was black and a good student. For various reasons, I don't have fond memories of that period. But that's all beside the point.

The important thing about those months is that with a lot of effort, or just because that's life and what can you do, I took my time, but eventually I got used to my new size. Little by little, I adjusted to that new body and learned to love it. A body with breasts that never did grow 'big enough', and with teeth an orthodontist later straightened slightly. My upper jaw and teeth don't stick out any more, but the teeth never came together in the supposedly perfect way I was promised. I was left with a diastema, and several other gaps where teeth were extracted to partly compensate for how toothy I looked. I had to learn to take more care than other people not to bang into things or break them. By the time I started eighth grade I felt more respected at school, and I felt like I'd earned it through my discipline. Up until eleventh grade, people still made fun of my hair a bit, saying it was like the mane of the lion on Channel A, because I sometimes wore it loose and it was curly. People teased me for being a virgin and said it caused cancer, that I should 'do it' with the one boyfriend I had while I was at school, who I was with for three months or so, not long before graduating. Of course, he broke up with me because I wouldn't. Then Fabio, one of my friends, used to say that chewing gum and corn arepas went together better than my outfits, because I wore skirts with T-shirts and trainers or hiking sandals, but by then I didn't care about the teasing. By then I was a young woman who laughed, loudly, showing off her sticking-out teeth and wild hair.

Later on, when I arrived in Medellín and started university, I went through something similar. I didn't feel comfortable in the spaces where my classmates hung out; I was used to meeting up to dance, and in Medellín people gathered to talk and drink. In the queue in the cafeteria, people used to pull my hair to see if it was real. I didn't really know how to dress now I was a student, and I always felt awkward. I only realise that now. The change wasn't so obvious in my body at that age, but essentially it was the same thing: I was growing.

Now Motete is growing, and since I'm in charge, or since, in a way, Motete and I are one and the same, I feel that familiar sense of measuring myself anew, getting to grips with my size all over again.

I'm not sure of the dimensions and that puts me at great risk of being clumsy, of stumbling and falling, but now falling doesn't just mean making my classmates laugh: it means risking what I've decided is my life's work.

I have a terrible fear of breaking things. And I worry that other things, like my clothes when I was twelve, don't fit me. It's scary not knowing how to divide my attention: I might waste time getting used to my new size, and meanwhile other situations might slip through my fingers.

In physical terms, Motete is bigger. We've taken the second floor of the building for another 500,000 pesos, and that's where we've put the kitchen for preparing snacks and lunches, as well as the offices and cake-making area. I have a lovely office, full of natural light, where I feel like I can think better, be by myself a little, read in peace. I'm just finishing making it beautiful.

I think a lot about which things we need to do and which we don't. About what we want to grow towards.

For now, I hope these growing pains, the kind that follow any big change, don't hit me too hard this time around.

Kisses and hugs,
Veliamar

Quibdó, 1 June 2018

On Tuesday I came back from Bahía Solano to get on with all the many things I do here. I'd gone there to vote and to see my grandma before my upcoming trip to Spain.

I wanted to write to you by hand when I got back, but there hasn't been time. For now I'm sending you some short letters that I wrote in my paradise. I didn't have any paper. And even if I had, it would be soaking wet. The humidity in that town is something else. All of us there are nothing but water.

Kisses.

Bahía Solano, 28 May 2018

Dear friend,

The sound of the many birds who live in this town is keeping me company at this hour. A lot has changed here: people speak openly about narcotrafficking now, and they know which families and which people work in the trade – a trade that sometimes seems more respectable than fishing or teaching. Transporting cocaine by boat is a family business – everyone's involved. Out in the street, the conversations have changed: people discuss kilos, journeys, who's in prison in Central America or the United States. Still, you can tell this land has a history of fighting oppression and knows plenty about resistance.

    Last night the moon came out where it always does. Radiant, it lit up the same balcony that was here in my childhood, which still contains pieces of timber from thirty-five years ago. The rain falls and makes a river of the earth, the street level rising and the houses seeming to sink inch by inch into the ground. And then neither the shiniest houses, nor the biggest, nor the ones adorned with marble sculptures as white as the product that pays for them, suggest anything close to growth or luxury. This is still a simple town, whose charm comes from the sea and the forest, only now the saltpetre carried in on the easterly winds doesn't erode

127

the usual materials, instead encountering bricks, tinted windows and high metal fences, which can't hold out forever and end up going the way of everything else around here: a little dilapidated, rather old, musty-smelling, with green stains spreading from each corner, and inhabited by tiny crabs that leave their own homes and move into people's houses.

As we've said before, this may be the Pacific, but it's not a peaceful place. Though I should add, my dear friend, that nothing brings me more peace than being here. There are things that come close, as you know: reading with the children, running FLECHO. But deep in my soul I have to accept that nothing and no one else stirs in me what I feel when I'm here. It's as if every time I inhale I'm taking the first breath of my life.

I walk on the beach at low tide and savour each step because my toes sink into the sand. I swim in the sea, though I prefer looking at it, and in the water I try to float and gaze at the sky, concentrating on the feeling of melting, of being just one tiny thing amid all this, which, I strongly believe, is what has shaped my way of seeing the world, and my character, and my relationship with the water and the land.

The fullness of my soul keeps the words from my lips. I feel I don't need them as much, and I fill up with silences. That's why I think the best way of telling you what's happening is for you to visit one day, so we can look together at this sea that here, unlike on the rest of the coast, always moves from north to south.

Hugs,
V.

Dear friend,

I've never asked for your permission to write. I just do it! You know that.

I've told you, and it's true, that I don't imagine your replies. I don't even expect them. Sometimes I want them because they make me happy. So all your replies are perfect. I know very little about your life beyond these letters, and I'm not curious.

I'm not interested in being part of the picture or learning about your real life. I even find it strange to hear your voice, because that's not the dimension in which I feel I relate to you. I wouldn't dial your number unless it was extremely urgent or necessary. A couple of times I've wanted to speak to you and then I've asked you directly, but that's rare.

I do feel that the practice of writing these words back and forth has an important place in my life. It inspires me, and gives me time to myself; I come back to the words over and over. Even so, we both know they don't have much to do with you, and only slightly more to do with me. It's really between my words and your answers.

You're very important, even indispensable. I don't think anyone else in the world would be prepared to do this, not with the reliable replies, or the open mind and sensitive approach that are, essentially, what make those replies 'perfect'.

People usually want either more or less than this. More would mean linking it to love in a concrete sense, talking about each other's lives, calling each other on the phone, meeting up, making promises, giving gifts; and less would mean intermittent, commitment-free friendship. Sporadic presences with no real bond. This is neither more nor less.

It's a kind of creation with no room for easy adjectives. I don't have you on my list of friends, but that's what I call you in every letter and you often behave as a great friend would behave. It seemed a loose definition because we're not such good friends really, yet you're much closer to me than many of my friends. You know what I mean. I won't keep trying to explain. We both know that some things are simply there and require no explanation.

This is an important part of my life and I want it to last a thousand years. I don't ever want a word from me to upset your real life. I imagine you happy, healthy and full of purpose. And imagining that is enough for me.

So let's stay here, my dear friend, in this sea which belongs to neither the north nor the south, which doesn't know where it's going because there's no need, which ebbs and flows, and is nothing but present yet knows what's behind it and carries on into the future.

I love you.

Quibdó, 30 July 2018

My dear friend,

In Cuenca I had a bout of something I haven't experienced for years and which is only now going away. Maybe because it's been such a dry summer, and probably all the more so because I live in the water and travelled to an arid place where I went twenty days without seeing the rain. Or maybe for emotional reasons, which I'll try to explain. Anyway, the point is, I got very bad dermatitis all over my hands and then grew a completely new skin, like a reptile.

It was tough at first, because I could hardly pick anything up, or type on the computer for very long. There came a time when I couldn't even touch my phone and had to wear gloves, as I did to carry my rucksack on the journey home.

My fingerprints disappeared completely. On one day, perhaps the most difficult, I couldn't even hold a pen. Having no fingerprints caused me a bit of trouble in Bogotá, and revealed the lack of humanity of some institutions. I couldn't collect the money my dad had wired me, even though I had my passport and my ID, it was obviously me and I had no way of solving the problem of my fingerprints. I had to wait at least ten days for my skin to grow back.

My skin is still peeling in places, and the new layer

remains very sensitive: if I'm hit by the corner of a hardback book, which has happened, my skin breaks a little or I get a small bruise. And aside from how painful it was, wherever I go people ask about my hands, even in airport security. In Quito they asked me to take off my gloves and then, well, they were pretty surprised and said sorry.

Lots of people kept on giving me diagnoses and prescriptions. At first I found it all a bit annoying, but then I began to embrace my change of skin, to understand it, even to love it. The time of stillness, silence and solitude in Cuenca was a pause that let me see my life from a distance; a pause to calm the many anxieties of the months that came before.

With my hands 'out of action', I was obliged to accept help from Margarita, the friend who put me up in Madrid, and then the Velia who's always so busy giving had to set about receiving instead.

Sometimes a change of skin can do you good.

A new skin, on my hands. So many symbols at once, you said over chat, and it stayed with me.

Hands for giving and receiving. For building. Losing your fingerprints, your identity. The pain of shedding your skin. The stillness and silence that lead to changes, movements and messages, so many messages from the body amid the silence and stillness. The new skin soft, delicate, transparent.

My dear friend,

I want to tell you lots of things, I always do, but there's no way I'll have time to tell you everything. These days I'm having a new sensation. Motete seems to be standing on its own two feet. I no longer feel as if I'm in training for something. I can sense fresh challenges ahead, and I'm not anxious about the same things. We have a new cash register and next week we'll have new accounting software. We're growing, no question. And my responsibilities are growing as well, and my time for other things I love is shrinking. Of course, everything taking up my time is completely fascinating to me.

I've thrown myself wholeheartedly into this work. The lack of effusiveness I mentioned a while back has taken up almost permanent residence within me. Aside from very rare moments, I've become more and more like that calm, deep bay. I can't deny the turbulence in the depths, but for the most part I'm fairly serene.

When it comes down to it, I don't think I need to tell you everything. I'm fine. It's all going well. What matters is not just making sure there's still time for poetry, but living constantly within it.

The most beautiful part is that I've stopped feeling as if I can't manage. I arrive in Medellín on October 24th, around midday. I'm free that evening. On Thursday and Friday I'll be at the National Reading Promoters' Conference. And I'm staying until the afternoon of Monday 29th. We could have breakfast that Monday, or on the Saturday.

Or we could have a drink on Wednesday evening. Let me know what's easiest for you.

Vel

Quibdó, 2 September 2018

I read your message, I reread it. I'm glad you're getting some rest. We won't meet up this time and I confess I felt sad when I read that. I feel sad now as I write it.

Medellín is more and more like a beloved memory. It's gradually fading away. I didn't think this would happen so quickly; three years isn't long. I suppose these letters stop it happening with you as well.

We'll have another chance soon enough, when some institution invites me to something. Then I'll go. And of course, I'll let you know. I have a present for you, and I wanted to give it to you in person. I think I'll keep it until we meet. Some things are meant for particular moments.

Hugs,
Velia

Director & Editor: Carolina Orloff
Director: Samuel McDowell

www.charcopress.com

Tidal Waters was published on
90gsm Munken Premium Cream paper.

The text was designed using Bembo 12 and ITC Galliard.

Printed in January 2024 by TJ Books
Padstow, Cornwall, PL28 8RW using responsibly
sourced paper and environmentally-friendly adhesive.